SWEETS AND SANTA

THE MATCHMAKING BAKER

ROSIE PEASE

PAISLEY PRESS BOOKS
WEST WARWICK, RHODE ISLAND

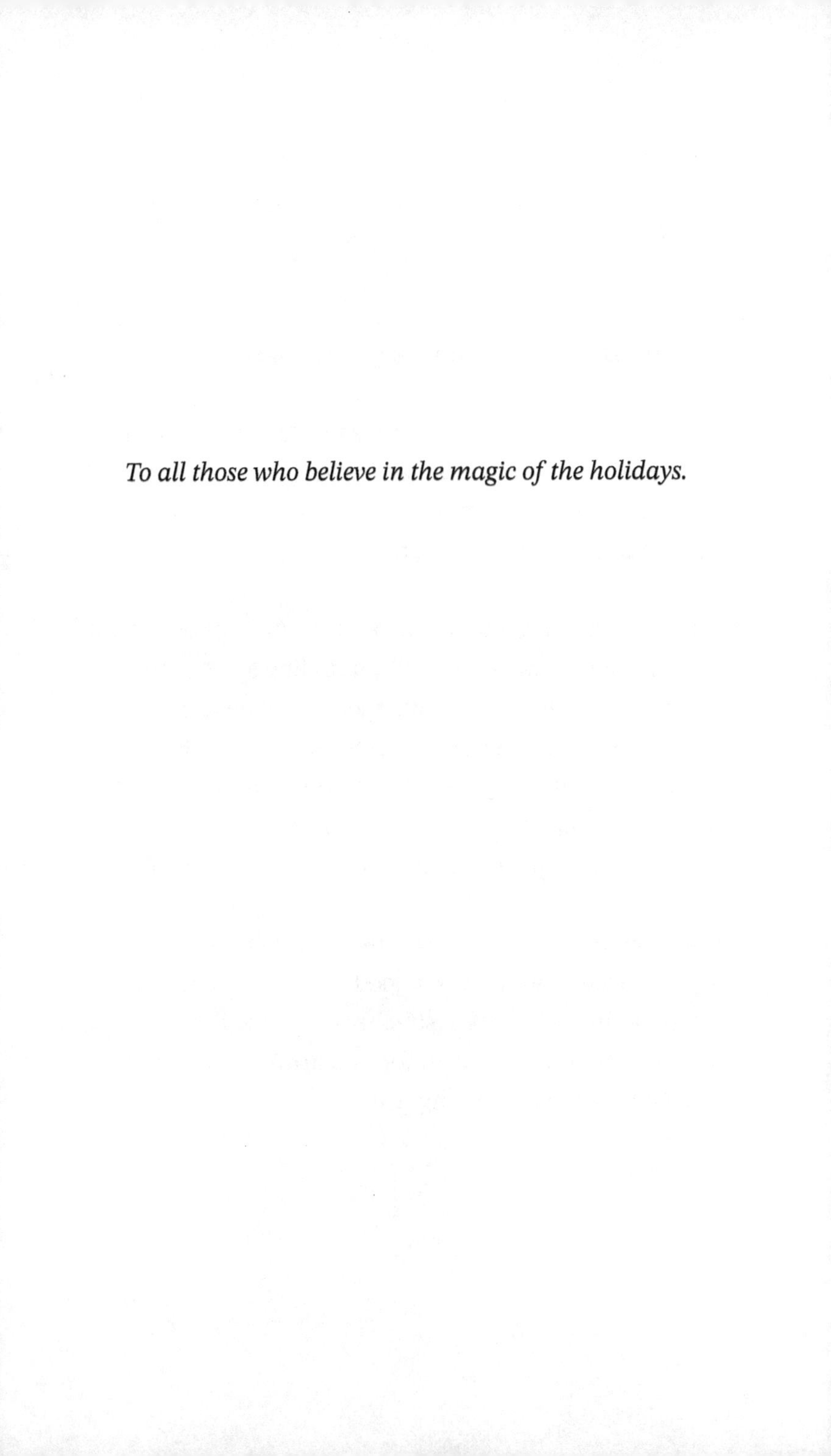

To all those who believe in the magic of the holidays.

ABOUT THIS BOOK

Christmas magic, mystery, and matchmaking.

Although my recipes are a perfect fit for the town Santa next door, without a budget for ads, I'm counting on word of mouth to drive business during my first Christmas as a bakery owner.

But as things around town start to disappear, it's all people can talk about as they wait in line for the jolly old elf. Rumors swirl as residents speculate whodunnit. And when one of the missing items is revealed to be an engagement ring last seen in my shop, my reputation is thrown in jeopardy. To save it, I'll have to crack this case wide open like the tops of my chocolate kringle cookies.

Will a bit of Christmas magic allow me to find the ring—along with the other stolen goods—and win over Heartwood Hollow with my festive treats? Or will my efforts for a sweet holiday season for all earn me a permanent place on the town's naughty list?

Author's Note

Dear Reader,

Thank you so much for picking *Sweets and Santa* as your next read. I loved writing this sweet holiday mystery to show some of my—and hopefully your—Heartwood Hollow favorites before the events in Mixing Up Magic. If you've read those books, I hope you enjoyed seeing a bit of an origin story for some of the characters. If you're new to my books, I hope you enjoy meeting these characters who you'll see again when you pick up the Mixing Up Magic books. It was fun being able to show this spin on Christmas magic before Joanie ever realizes that there's more to herself and Heartwood Hollow than meets the eye.

I love hearing from my readers. If you'd like to reach out to me, you can find me throughout social media @WriteRosiePease.

Happy reading!

Cheers,

Rosie

CHAPTER 1

The cottage appeared overnight as if by magic in Founder's Park, the little postage stamp of a park next to my bakery. It was my second holiday season in Heartwood Hollow but the first with my bakery open. Last year at this time, I had only been in town a couple months and was renovating the space I'd leased to convert it from a florist to a bakery. Suncraft Bakery. *My* bakery. One that had been a dream of mine to open since childhood.

So although I'd seen Santa's house last year, I didn't get to experience the full magic of it day in and day out like I was about to. The arrival of the cottage signaled the true start of the holiday season in town with small events happening almost daily, culminating in Santa's arrival the following weekend, complete with a town parade, carolers, and of course, food.

I couldn't wait to experience it all.

The only thing that would have made the cottage more magical was some snow, but there was nothing in the forecast for the next several days despite temperatures being cold enough for it. The town would likely put down fake snow or truck in real stuff from farther upstate where the mountains already had plenty.

I couldn't resist peeking inside the cottage before I unlocked the bakery. I was early anyway, the benefit of living in an apartment on Main Street a few hundred feet from where I worked. My team wasn't due in for several more minutes, so I brought my face close to the glass, putting my hand up to try to block the minimal glare from the two streetlights bordering the park. Inside, I could just make out the plush wing-back chair where Santa would sit with kids climbing onto his lap to tell him they'd been good children this year and what they'd like to see under the tree. A fireplace stood a few feet away, fake most likely. It hadn't been lit last year. There was a table with a small printer that would spit out photos of the kids and Santa, a free keepsake offered by the town, although parents could pay for more photos or larger print sizes. Next to the printer on the table sat a cute little gnome, its hat pulled down over its eyes. I wondered if whoever took the photos used it to get kids' attention so they could snap the perfect picture.

Soon there would be a line out the cottage door. Hopefully many of the kids from that line would then find their way through the door to the bakery.

It was my favorite time of year for baking. I'd been playing with new recipes for a few weeks now, perfecting a holiday lineup. Peppermint cookies with crushed candy canes, cranberry orange cookies, gingerbread men, sugar cookies dipped in white chocolate then decorated to look like snow globes, and more. Today was the first time they'd be sold in the shop, and I couldn't wait to get started. Ready to start the day, I headed to the back door of the bakery and unlocked it. I flipped on the light switch, taking in the kitchen I'd worked so hard to make mine. It only had three stations, but if this season went well enough, I'd be able to take on another baker.

As I set my bag in the drawer at my station, the door opened, revealing Gina and Bryan, my bakers. Gina had been with me since a few weeks after the bakery opened. Bryan came on mid-summer. I didn't know much of their backstories yet, but they were both from here, although Gina had spent some time away. Bryan had come to me after it didn't work out at one of the restaurants on Main Street. I'd been told he was a good worker but had butted heads with another cook. Each cook had believed they'd known better, and even though Bryan actually did know better, according to his former boss, the others on the staff had soured against Bryan, so he was the one to go. So far, I hadn't seen any behavior like what had been described, but as I told both Bryan and Gina when they came here, this wasn't just a job. It was a team and a family too.

"Morning, Joanie," Bryan said, Gina echoing the same a little softer.

"Morning, you two. Did you see the cottage next to the shop? Things are about to get busy here, so I hope you are ready."

"Absolutely," Gina replied. "The busier the better."

"So what are we working on today?" Bryan asked, taking off his coat and then sticking it in the closet.

"We have the usual muffins for the diner, and Libby is offering her first holiday tea and has asked for a bit of help with that, so we're making cookies for her. Once we're done with the regular shop offerings, cookies are all we are working on. They are going to be huge this week and all the way through Christmas."

Bryan and Gina swapped spots at the closet. Gina tucked her hat into the sleeve of her coat before hanging it up. "Sounds good to me. I love a good Christmas cookie."

I chuckled. "Oh, I'm not settling for good. They will be great cookies." They had to be.

Gina nodded hard once, then returned to her worktable. She was on scone duty, while Bryan was doing the muffins. I had cupcakes. We didn't go much beyond this for our regular daily menu, but for the holidays, I had an expanded order ahead menu that included pies, pastries, specialty cakes, and other holiday favorites like yule logs and even fruit cake. But the cookies were by far what would put us over the top.

Shortly before six, I loaded my bike with a muffin delivery for Olde Templeton and Double Aitch diners. My stops at Double Aitch were always quick and uncomplicated, but Olde Templeton had a chance of taking a while.

"I can't believe you're still makin' deliveries on your bike," Donna said when I walked into the tiny eatery. Olde Templeton was small but cozy with the typical diner vibe and a cup of hot coffee on the counter waiting for me. Its appearance meant Donna had something she wanted to tell me.

I slid up onto the counter stool, placing the boxes of muffins next to the coffee mug. "It's a bit cold, but the biking warms me up." I took off my hat and gloves, then picked up the mug. "As does the coffee." I'd never been much for black coffee, but with a bit of half and half—which also helped it cool down to a drinkable tempera-ture—it wasn't that bad. Especially on a cold morning like this.

Donna leaned against the counter, a stray brown and silver curl of hair falling in front of her face. She pushed it back behind her ear. "And what are you gonna do when it finally snows?"

"My station wagon is fully outfitted for any type of delivery." I'd installed the extra straps and buckles all around the floor of the trunk to help keep boxes and cake boards in place. I had no doubt whatever I put in the back of my car would be secure back there.

"Could happen any day now according to my knee." She grabbed her specials whiteboard from the wall, then popped the cap off a dry erase marker. "So what did you bring today?"

She scribbled furiously as I rattled off the six-flavor list, then as she was popping the lid back onto her marker said, "So I hear Heartwood Hollow is about to have another newly engaged couple, and I have it under good authority that this one is, once again, thanks to you."

"Oh, really? Who?" I had a pretty good idea consid-ering I'd only matched three couples in town so far, one of which still felt too new to be getting engaged. The other had been engaged since September.

"Well," Donna began, and I sipped my coffee as she continued, "Walter told me that his wife, Martha, told him that Greta from the historical society saw Drew Craig at Baubles and Bangles lookin' at rings. And when I asked his grandmother, she confirmed that he'd bought one. He's such a nice boy, I'm glad Megan makes him so happy."

"They're a great couple." Their match had been instantaneous upon their seeing one another, one of the fastest and strongest I'd ever felt.

"I think Tricia over at Baubles should start giving you commissions. One is a coincidence, might even argue that a second one is too, but I know you got Carl and Beth together earlier this summer too. They'd briefly been sweethearts in high school, but both of them have been gone a few years. Never thought I'd see the two of them together again."

That must have explained the way their match vibrated through me when it struck. It was weak at first, thready but there. Beth had been hesitant when I said she should go for it. I wondered what had caused them to stop being high school sweethearts. It couldn't have been too major for the match to still be present on both sides. It wasn't remotely close to what I believed a broken match felt like.

"Well, I think they make a wonderful couple. I happened to be at the right place at the right time to give them a bit of a shove, that's all." A big shove.

Donna quirked an eyebrow at me. "People are already talking about you and how you should set up shop as a matchmaker in addition to your baking.

Doesn't help much that the kids at the high school are asking for your muffins before they go take tests, swearin' they're good luck. You ready for that? Finals are coming up."

"Well, my muffins *are* good, but I don't know about good luck." I took another sip of my coffee, a chuckle playing at my lips.

Donna held up a hand. "Just telling you what I heard, but since the school year picked back up, I've had more requests for grilled muffins to go from students than I ever did. That's why I had to increase my order with you, and I've not had a problem with getting rid of them all before lunch."

I shrugged, grateful that was all the rumors about me said. I could handle being known as a matchmaker. People could accept that as me being good at setting others up. That was how it was in high school when I would convince friends to dance with one another or suggest to a guy that they should ask a particular girl to dance. The same happened at parties in college. Few people thought anything of it.

I wasn't the first matchmaker in my family. My mom could do it too. She'd matched plenty of people through their love of books and at various programs held by the library where she worked. I'd grown up watching her do it, so it only made sense that I had picked up a few of her people skills. The tingling I felt was just some weird sensation I must have developed as a way to decide who should be with whom. Mom said she felt tingles too. Like mother, like daughter, right?

Donna rapped on the counter. "I should probably let

you go. You must have a lot going on with the upcoming Christmas festivities."

I took one last sip of my coffee, then pulled my wallet out of my purse. "Thanks, Donna. It was good to chat with you."

She held up her hand. "You know I'm not gonna charge you for the coffee."

Slipping the wallet back in my bag, I nodded. "Thanks again." I stood up off the stool, then headed out the diner.

"Hello, Joanie," Walter said as he and his best friend Paul passed me on their way into Olde Templeton. The two old men were regulars, and it wasn't uncommon for me to run into them in the mornings, especially on days when Donna bribed me with coffee to stay and chat.

"Have a good one, fellas." I gave them a small wave before walking around the side of the building where I stowed my bike and trailer to keep it out of the way and a little hidden from anyone passing by on Main Street.

I rode back to the bakery thinking about what Donna had said. Rumors were spreading through town about me. She wasn't the first one to bring it up. Sarah, my shop assistant, had said as much a few times. It didn't bother me so much. If people wanted to think my muffins were good luck, who was I to argue? I welcomed them if it meant more people would stop by the shop to buy things. Who wouldn't want that?

Besides, the rumors could have been a lot worse.

They could have been about my biggest secret. The one thing I could do that made me different. It went way beyond matchmaking. I'd only ever told one friend about my ability and it ended the friendship I'd had since kindergarten. To this day, I didn't think Ginny had ever told anyone what she knew, likely no one would believe her, but losing my closest friend as a young teen meant I'd probably never tell another soul about what I could do.

Living soul, anyway.

The ghosts only I could see had ways of figuring my ability out on their own, especially when they caught me off guard. There had been some surprises over the years, but they were few and far between. I'd been careful since moving to Heartwood Hollow, and for a place that was crawling with ghosts, I'd done a fairly good job of pretending they weren't there. And they'd done the same for me.

I pulled into the parking lot behind the bakery, then secured my bike and trailer to a parking pylon close to the door.

Gina and Bryan were just finishing their last batches of breakfast goods as I walked back into the kitchen.

I clapped my hands. "Let's make some cookies."

CHAPTER 2

After doing a quick survey of supplies we had upstairs, I headed into the basement where we stored surplus ingredients. With as many cookies as we were going to be making, I needed to grab more sugar and our entire stock of chocolate chips. We'd used up what was left in the kitchen on the muffins and scones this morning.

"All right, you two," I said when I reentered the kitchen. "I need one of you on sugar cookie dough, the other on chocolate. I'll take peanut butter. Quadruple the recipe."

"Quadruple?" Gina's eyes widened. "Joanie, are you sure? That's a lot of sugar cookies."

"Yeah," Bryan agreed. "They're great and everything, but don't you think it's a little plain?"

I smiled mischievously as I pulled peanut butter off the shelf and plopped it on my table. "Have I steered either of you wrong yet?"

The two shook their heads, Bryan muttering a *no* as they each got to work.

"When you're done"—I scooped out a cup of sugar and dumped it into my mixing bowl—"let me know. I have new recipes for you to make from those."

"Should have known this was only going to be base dough."

Next came brown sugar for my cookies. "You got it. Each dough will make four varieties of cookies, none of them plain today. You two are going to love the lineup this season."

I could have sworn the lights in the kitchen brightened ever so slightly.

"A little excited there, aren't you, Joanie?" Bryan chuckled.

I nodded enthusiastically. "I have been waiting for Christmas since opening the shop and saving recipes for a long time." They didn't know it yet, but the cookies would be completely different tomorrow and throughout the week. I'd go off this week's sales and requests from customers to decide what we'd be making for the big event Saturday when Santa came to town.

When their doughs were done, I handed recipe cards for what to do with each portion.

Gina *mmm*ed before she was through the second side, and based on how quickly the reaction started, Bryan was licking his lips by the second line on the front of his card.

The two of them made me laugh. They reminded me of the kids who would come into the bakery so eager to get a sweet treat that they'd press their faces against the glass. The cases were my favorite thing to clean because of this. I loved seeing the proof of how much excitement and joy my baked goods brought people.

Still chuckling, I turned back to my workstation and added in a few pinches of salt. I pushed the large bowl of sugar and salt aside, then grabbed a smaller bowl. I hurried to the fridge for my eggs. One by one, I cracked the eggs into the smaller bowl and poured the contents into my mixing bowl. The last thing I wanted was to get eggshells in the mix by breaking the eggs into it directly or to ruin the whole batch by finding a bad egg after it had already been dumped on top of everything.

I brought the large mixing bowl over to my stand mixer and set it on the platform, then as I brought the mixer up to speed, in went the flour, followed by softened butter, and finally the peanut butter. A smaller batch I could have done by hand, but for the sake of still needing to use my arms today, this much peanut butter and flour was too much. When everything was mixed, I grabbed my bowl and returned to my workstation, allowing Gina access to the mixer for her sugar cookies.

I dumped the dough onto my station and formed it into one long log, then broke that into four separate chunks and placed three back in the mixing bowl. At this rate, I was going to need larger tables. Of the three I'd put aside, one would become thumbprint cookies with large chocolate chips pressed into their centers. Another would become a jelly thumbprint, and the next I was rolling into crushed peanut butter candies before setting them onto a tray to bake. Right now I was working on a batch that I'd make like traditional peanut butter cookies, a fork pressed into them to flatten them, but they'd be turned into sandwiches for a chocolate cream when they were done baking.

Once the first two trays were full, I brought them to the oven and slid them in, sharing space with Gina and Bryan who were almost matching me in speed batch for batch. It worked best this way anyway as it guaranteed the cases would be stocked with a variety of each type by the time the shop was ready to open.

I glanced at the clock. Sarah would be here soon. She couldn't bake—at all. I'd told her to give it a try one afternoon just to see if it were possible to train her, and we'd decided that wouldn't work out for either of us, but she kept the front end working smoothly and was an indispensable part of the team. It was a shame I couldn't give her more than a couple days a week right now. She worked at the bank when she wasn't here. If this Christmas season exceeded expectations, in addition to hiring another baker, I hoped to add another day to Sarah's work schedule too. She was that good at what she did. Plus, having her here allowed me more freedom to come and go between the bakeshop and the kitchen as needed or to make a last-minute delivery.

Through the window in the door separating the two spaces, I watched the lights flick on. A moment later, Sarah breezed into the kitchen to put away her things, her face pink from the cold.

"Stand by the oven for a minute if you need to warm up," I said as I walked over to it with another one of my finished cookie trays. "It's gonna be open for a few as we swap out trays. I hope you're ready for cookies galore."

"You think I'd be used to the cold having lived here my whole life, but when it comes around again, I never am." She followed me to the oven. "Give me a few weeks, and I'll be acclimated."

Saying nothing about how there had already been a couple weeks of weather like this, I passed her the uncooked tray as I opened the oven door, then slid on mitts to pull out the baked cookies.

"Oh, these smell so good. I can't wait to try them. I promised my grandfather I'd bring some to him too. He's very familiar with your usual offerings but has been looking forward to the cookies you've been teasing."

"Well, I hope he's hungry." I set a finished tray on a rack to cool, then reached in for another from the oven. "There are going to be new cookies all week."

"Speaking of, you took into account today your special order at the inn?"

I nodded. "Yeah. Once these go in the oven, I'll see what time it is. We can probably make a few extra just in case."

"This is big news, Joanie. I don't know if you realize that. Libby's teas draw from all around the area, and she usually does it all herself."

"It's just one tea . . ."

"But you never know. It could open more doors for you. Libby's got a lot of connections, and then there's the whole tourist factor to consider. They have your stuff there today and they stop by before they go home."

I pulled the last tray from the oven and then put it on the cooling rack. "No pressure."

She flapped a hand at me. "Pssh! You'll be fine."

I took the tray she'd been holding and slid it into the oven, then turned to take the waiting trays from Gina and Bryan. Sarah slipped into the shop to prepare it for opening. I'd go in and help her in a few minutes, but first I had to prep the next stage for the sandwich cookies. I mixed some confectioners' sugar into peanut butter. This way, the peanut butter would be sweeter and creamier when we spread it onto the chocolate cookies Bryan had made.

"Bryan, will you melt down some chocolate, and Gina, let's get a chocolate cream going. There are a bowl and beaters already chilling in the freezer for it." I'd put them there last night so the cream would be more stable after it was whipped.

Once the first batch of cookies had cooled enough, I told Bryan to pour the melted chocolate into two bowls and to get another round started. He had it handled and started dipping the cranberry orange cookies Gina made into one bowl so that half of each was covered with chocolate.

Gina, done with the chocolate cream, spread dollops of it onto the peanut butter cookies to make sandwiches with it. When she offered to do the reverse with the chocolate cookies and peanut butter cream, I ducked into the shop, taking a tray of cookies that didn't need extra treatment with me.

"You see the Christmas cottage went up in the park overnight?" I asked.

"Kind of hard to miss it." Sarah didn't look up from stocking the cash register. She sighed wistfully. "I do love it so. Every year is a little different. Have you figured out a design yet for the window decorating contest?"

I opened one of the cases, then slid the tray inside. "Not yet. I was planning on taking Tuesday to go shopping for things and decorating on Wednesday." I rearranged the cookies on the tray to make more room so we could reuse some of the other trays for the second round of baking.

"You mean to tell me you have had your cookies planned out for months, but you've given no thought to how you'd decorate your windows?" Now she turned to give me an incredulous stare. "You've seen them done throughout town for all the major holiday seasons, including this one, so it's not like you didn't know."

I told Sarah to hold that thought as I ducked into the kitchen for another tray. When I returned, she was writing tags for the day's flavors of baked goods.

"It's not that I haven't thought of anything." I plopped the next tray on top of the case. "It's that I've thought of too much!"

Gina stepped into the bakeshop, a tray of scones in her hand. "I'd think you have the perfect window display opportunity built in."

Out of the corner of my eye, I could see Sarah cock her head to the side.

"What?" Gina shrugged. "Neither of you were talking quietly about it. I could hear you when the doors were open."

"So what was your idea?" I asked, taking the cookies from one tray and putting them on the other already inside the case.

Sarah slid the case next to mine open, and Gina placed her tray inside. "Cookies for Santa, of course."

"I thought of that," I said, emptying my tray, "but don't you think that's a little predictable?"

Gina turned and headed back into the kitchen, holding the door open for me. "All depends on the delivery, I guess."

"That's true, I suppose."

She passed me a tray from the cooling rack, then took one for her. Bryan was nearly done dipping the chocolate peanut butter cookie sandwiches in chocolate, sprinkling crushed peanut butter cups over the melted chocolate before it had time to fully set. Someday it would be nice to be able to make everything that we added to our cookies, but until that day came, we'd have to settle for store-bought.

"I'm sure you could find a good way to spin it or add elements that the judges wouldn't be thinking of." She followed me back into the kitchen. "Kind of a give them what they expect in an unexpected way."

"Hmm . . . You could be on to something. We'll see what I find to work with on Tuesday."

The rest of the morning flowed smoothly. The uptick in foot traffic for the holidays was already noticeable, which hopefully was a precursor for the entire season. Best of all, Libby from the inn was thrilled with the cookies I'd brought her, impressed with both the flavor variety and quantity . . . I may have brought her a few more than she'd ordered so she and her husband could try them, hoping they'd keep me in mind for future events or just to recommend me to her guests in the future for things.

I hadn't expected it to work so quickly.

The phone rang as I was getting cleaning supplies ready for closing. It stopped after only one ring, so Sarah must have picked it up.

Less than a minute later, she stuck her head into the kitchen. "Joanie, it's for you. Libby from the inn."

"I'll pick it up in here, thanks." I stood the broom against the wall, then hurried to the phone. "Hi, Libby. It's Joanie. How are you?"

"Oh, good. Real good. Listen, I just wanted to thank you again for coming to my rescue today with the cookies for my holiday tea. It truly took a load off."

"You're welcome. I hope they went over well."

"People raved about them. A total hit. And they were good . . . not that I got to try many of them after Billy absconded with the small box you brought just for us."

I couldn't help but smile. "I'm so glad. It's always great to hear positive reviews."

"Well, that's why I'm calling. Everyone loved them so much that I'm hoping you could help me with the tea I'm having on Wednesday. Not as formal as this holiday tea was, but enough. I'm still just swamped with getting the inn set up for the holiday—we're hosting a tree trimming in our foyer that evening—and it would really help me out."

"Wednesday, you said?"

"You sound uncertain." Drats, I'd hoped to hide the reaction. "Is that going to be a problem?"

"Well, we're usually closed Tuesdays and Wednesdays . . ."

"Oh, I couldn't ask you to come in for just my tea service." She sounded horrified by the thought. "I'm sure I'll manage."

"No, no. It's fine." I waved off her worries as if she could see me. "I was planning on coming in on Wednesday anyway to work on the window display. It won't be a problem to whip up a couple batches for you."

Libby let out a big sigh of relief. "You are a lifesaver."

We chatted a few more minutes about what cookies she'd want so I could get supplies for the unexpected order, and since it was all I'd be making, I could tailor it to her preferences. After we hung up, I grabbed the broom and dustpan once more, then brought it out to the shop.

Sarah looked up from wiping down the back counter. "What did Libby want? Did everything go okay with her tea?"

"It was great, actually. She put in another order for Wednesday."

She raised an eyebrow. "But the bakery is closed."

I shrugged. "It won't be a problem considering I was already planning on being here."

"Should you ask Gina or Bryan to come in?"

Shaking my head as I started to sweep, I said, "It should be fine. I used to make that many cookies by myself all the time." My gram had a large circle of friends, *the ladies* as she called them. When I was little, I made her cookies to take with her when she visited them. And I was always the one offering to bring cookies in for class parties. Libby's order was one I could do in my sleep.

At that moment, the shop door opened, and when I looked up to see who had entered, Drew was hurrying inside. Momentarily my smile brightened, assuming he was likely here to tell me he was going to ask Megan to marry him, but it faltered as I realized he did *not* look like a man excited about proposing.

Something had gone wrong, but what?

CHAPTER 3

"Drew, what's wrong?"

The lights dimmed, almost as if in reaction to the feeling in the room. I had no idea why they did that. The building had been given a clean bill of health by the inspector when I leased the place and multiple times throughout renovations. When it first happened, brightening one day to where even the few customers inside the store noticed, I called an electrician to check everything out. Nothing. The shop's electricity was perfectly fine.

Drew stopped a few feet in front of me. "Is it here?"

"Is what here?" I had no idea what he was talking about.

"The ring. I came here earlier to show you the ring I plan on proposing to Megan with, and now it's is missing. I can't find it anywhere." He rubbed the sides of his face with both hands, pulling his cheeks down each time. "I take it by your reaction when I walked in that you don't have it."

I glanced at Sarah to confirm, and her wide eyes and unsure grimace told me all I needed to know. Looking back at Drew, I shook my head. "I'm sorry, but no."

"What am I going to do? I've been planning to propose on Saturday, but I can't do that without a ring."

"I'm sure it will turn up. Look, we're starting to clean up for the day. Maybe we just haven't found it yet. I will call you if it shows up."

"Can you call me either way? I know part of me will be wondering."

"I will. But in the meantime, where else have you been?"

"I'm on my way to all of those places now. But I took it out here, so I had to check with you first." He sighed and dropped his head. "Thanks, Joanie."

"Hey, Drew?" He looked up, a shred of hope in his eyes. "It will turn up."

Nodding, he slowly turned away from me and trudged out of the bakery.

"Poor guy," Sarah said. "I'd meant to say he'd been here earlier when you were out making your delivery. He was so excited."

"I should have offered him a cookie. Cookies make everything better. Even if just for a short while."

"Shouldn't you be getting ready to go?"

I glanced at Sarah, who was tapping at her wrist where a watch would be. She pointed to the clock.

"You have to meet your realtor at five and you walked here."

"Drats." She was right. I'd have just enough time to

get to the house if I left in the next minute. "Are you sure you can handle closing?"

"Yes, now go." She made a shooing motion with her hands.

I rested the broom against the case, thanking Sarah profusely for the reminder. I ran to grab my coat from the kitchen closet, then back into the shop. Sarah handed me my bag from under the counter, and I rushed out the door.

Steph and Alex were at my door within minutes of me arriving back home.

"Come on in," I called, not wanting to get out of my cushy chair I'd flopped into. I closed my book, placing it on the end table next to the chair. Saffy, my calico cat, barely lifted her head to acknowledge my friends' entrance. She was used to this routine by now.

Steph, a junior reporter with the town newspaper, and Alex, an assistant football coach at the high school were twins who lived across the hall from me in our Main Street apartment that sat above the local insurance agency. We'd met the day I moved in when Steph knocked on the door, smelling something weird coming from the apartment. She came face to face with me, a book in my hand, with my gram and mom waving smoking sage bundles around in the air to smudge the place and clean it of negative energies. Not my thing, but it made them feel good and kept them out of my stuff as I unpacked. However, nothing kept

Saffy from my unpacking. She was having the best time jumping from one empty box to another as I unpacked my bookshelf. Steph took my new-agey family and sassy cat in stride, however, and we'd been friends ever since.

Steph sat on the end of the couch closest to me. "How'd the showing go today?"

I let my head fall back against the chair.

"Not a winner, I take it?" Alex asked from the far corner of the couch, spreading his long legs out in front of him and reaching up to scratch Saffy's neck.

"Too much to do to it to make it mine. I want something a little more move-in friendly." I chuckled. "I'm not over all the work I had to do to the bakery yet."

"You'll find a place soon. There's not a ton around here, we tend to stick around if you haven't noticed, but something will turn up."

I didn't blame people for not leaving. I'd fallen in love with Heartwood Hollow's charm the moment Mom and I rolled onto Main Street. "I hope so. Thank goodness Ed was cool with a month-to-month lease. There was no way I could afford to lose my deposit by breaking a year-long lease. I really want a decent kitchen and a little more room to move around in. I don't know how you two do it with both of you living in your place."

Steph and Alex exchanged a glance I didn't understand, but I chalked it up to some sort of twin thing. Finally, Steph shrugged. "We try to get outside as often as we can."

"And we use the kitchen sparingly," Alex added. "We might not be great chefs like you, but we agree that it doesn't have everything. Speaking of food, what are we doing for dinner?"

I wiggled deeper into my spot. "All I know is I'm not making it tonight. I'm out of ideas after trying to figure out what I'm doing for the holiday window display at the bakery."

"How about cheese?"

I scrunched my face. "Doesn't really fit with the bakery. Pretty sure Louise has that covered."

A wide smirk spread across Alex's face. "Grilled cheese. For dinner. We can call and I'll go pick it up. Gotta get rid of this nervous energy. Big game coming up this weekend after the parade, and I'm trying some new drills to get us prepared."

"Oh, that's right. What do you think your odds are?" The team here wasn't the greatest, but there was tons of school spirit.

Alex shrugged. "We'll see. It would be great to win this one. We were so close to beating Knoll's Grove at homecoming, I'd love to do it this time."

"Well, I wish you and the boys good luck."

"Think you could make some muffins for us?"

"Sure! I'll have them ready for you before the parade. Just let me know how many you need." I thought for a second. "Wait, don't tell me you buy into that good luck muffin nonsense too."

Alex burst out in laughter. "Me? No. But a few of the kids on the team talked about getting good grades on a test after not studying or anything. The only thing they did differently was have one of your muffins that morning from the diner."

"That's just a coincidence," I stated. Donna and her muffin theory was one thing, but now my friends were mentioning it too?

"I figured it couldn't hurt, though," he replied with a shrug. "If that's what takes for them to think they can win, then why not?"

A pillow smacked against the side of his head. "All right, enough about the muffins. Let's talk grilled cheese. I'm hungry." Steph pulled out her phone. "Ugh. I forgot you somehow don't get cell service in here. Hang on. I have a paper menu in our apartment."

She jogged out of my apartment and returned a moment later with the menu. She handed the menu to me along with a small spiral-bound notebook and a pen, looking very reporterly. "Here. I already picked out what I want."

I glanced through the menu, settling on an apple, brie, and spinach grilled cheese on a multigrain loaf, before passing the menu to Alex.

"Oh, and a side of their cheese curds," Steph said.

"That sounds good. Me too," I added.

"Okay . . . four orders of cheese curds." Alex scribbled it into the notebook. Steph raised an eyebrow at him. As if he could feel her reaction—and maybe he could through some sort of twin thing—without looking up, he replied, "What? I'm a growing boy. You know, gotta grow up tall and strong."

She brought her hand up to cover her face and slowly shook her head.

We called and placed an order, and twenty minutes later, Alex walked to Cheese Louise to pick it up like he'd offered. It was only two buildings away, so he was back in no time.

"I heard the strangest thing as I was walking to grab the sandwiches," Alex said as we sat down to my small table to eat. I couldn't wait to have a larger table someday.

"Oh yeah?"

"You know the chef statue outside Salvatore's that holds the specials board?" Steph and I both nodded as Alex opened the large brown paper bag with our food in it. "His chef hat and apron are missing."

"It's not the first time his hat has gone missing," Steph said, reaching into the bag for her to-go container. "I swear it disappears at least once a year. It's got to be a prank that kids are playing or something. But who would want that beat up apron? It's been tied to that statue for years."

I knew a thing or two about aprons. "If it was as ratty as you say, could it have finally just fallen off? The ties can rip off the apron if they get too worn."

Taking the bag from his sister, Alex shook his head. "Not from the way even the people at Cheese Louise were talking. Seems Mr. Sal thinks it was stolen."

"I repeat," Steph began as she popped the lid off the container holding her order or cheese curds, "who would want that dirty thing?"

Alex shrugged, then handed me the containers holding my sandwich and cheese curds. "I'm sure you'll hear more about it at work. Guess Mr. Sal even filed a police report."

"All this apron talk reminds me . . . I was in such a

rush to meet with my realtor and get to the open house this evening that I left the bakery wearing my apron under my coat. I didn't even realize it until Kathy told me. Ugh! Talk about embarrassing."

Steph laughed, nearly causing herself to choke on a cheese curd, which only made her laugh harder. "Only you, Joanie. Only you."

"Thank goodness for Sarah. I never would have remembered the open house today if she weren't there."

Alex nodded. "You're lucky you found her when you did. She's always been organized. Even back in elementary school."

Being new to it, I forgot how intertwined this town was. It always surprised me when someone said they knew someone else I did. Even though Sunny Valley, where I'd grown up, was small, it hadn't seemed as tightly woven.

"And always prepared for anything too," Steph added.

"I completely agree." I told them of my hopes to add another day to her schedule. They thought that sounded great, and conversation soon shifted. All thoughts of stolen aprons, missing engagement rings, and magic muffins drifted away.

The next morning, there was a notice in the paper about the apron from Salvatore's, no mention of the hat. If it went missing as often as Steph said it did, maybe Mr. Sal was used to it. I thought briefly that Drew should take out an ad about the ring, but would have ruined any chance he still had at surprising Megan. Next to the notice of the apron was a note about a missing lawn ornament. I'd seen the dog statue a few streets off Main while making various deliveries over the several months the bakery had been open, and the owner was a regular customer. She always dressed up the statue for the holiday. A green leprechaun hat for St. Patrick's Day, sunglasses in an American flag motif for the Fourth of July. Last year for Christmas, it had a Santa hat and beard. I'm sure the owner missed it.

What in the world was happening in Heartwood Hollow that these things were suddenly going missing?

CHAPTER 4

"Did you hear about the dog statue?" I asked Sarah as she and I loaded the cases on Monday morning. It and the apron were all anyone could talk about in the kitchen, and Donna had been keen to talk about it as I dropped off her muffins.

"Can't imagine why someone would want either of those things, but Clara is devastated Stay is gone. Her husband started decorating it years ago, and now that he's gone, she's been doing it in his memory."

"Stay?"

"Yeah. Like sit and stay. He's Stay because he's a statue and can't go anywhere. Or at least he shouldn't have been able to go anywhere." Sarah sighed. "I have just as many photos with that dog at Christmas as I do with Santa at his cottage."

I pushed the cookies on the tray toward the front end to make room for more. "Wow. I had no idea it was that big of a deal."

"Speaking of decorating things, any more thought to what you're doing for the windows?"

"No." The word came out as a half groan as I stood. I returned to the kitchen, motioning for Sarah to follow. She did and I passed her a tray from the cooling rack before grabbing one for myself. "Maybe I will just do cookies for Santa this year. It's only my first year, so this is probably the best time to do it. Any other year it might seem like I'm falling back on the obvious. Then next year I can start early. I'll have a better handle on what cookies I'll be making instead of having focused on those like this year."

Tray in hand, Sarah held the door for me with her foot as we headed back into the shop. "Sounds like a plan to me."

People bustled in and out all morning. I could only imagine how it would be during the height of the season once school let out for a couple weeks. Busy with the shop's renovations last year, I couldn't remember quite how much traffic Main Street got during the day. I'd only been aware of how busy the events were at night. As a new shop owner, I'd gone to each one hoping to network with as many people as I could. I'd even rented time at a commercial kitchen in Snowhaven, the small city about a half hour away, to make a few sweet treats to pass out during the Stroll Along Main Street. Usually a Thursday once a month, strolls were more frequent during the holiday season. It wasn't uncommon to see tables out in front of stores with samples of things at any holiday town event, depending on the weather, of course. The one exception to that was the opening holiday parade. The sidewalks were too full of onlookers to set up a spot or even to go from one table to another. No one moved during the parade, so much so that I planned to close down during the event this year and would open back up once Santa arrived at his cottage next door, signaling everyone to disperse.

I made my way up Main Street, grateful that, with my bike, I could ride on the street. The sidewalks were bustling, and had I tried to make this delivery on foot, I easily would have been knocked into at least a couple of times.

Town Hall sat tucked away off Main Street. Its front lawn was officially part of the streetscape, but the building itself sat further back. I assumed it had been behind some storefronts originally, but those buildings had been torn down either out of necessity or to create the lawn.

Right now, the lawn was teeming with curious little creatures. Squat with bulbous noses and hats that were pulled down to those noses. Only some looked to have eyes, the bottoms of which were peeking out from under the brims of the tall pointy hats in various darker shades of red, green, and gray. The occasional one had a hat sitting higher on their heads as if they'd just pushed the hats out of their faces but were resigned to the hat's inevitable falling back down. All told, the fifty-some-odd gnomes each only came up to my knee and appeared haphazardly placed, few looking toward exactly the same spot.

I wove my way around the gnomes toward the front entrance. The stately building had large marble steps, taller than standard.

I'd slipped on them once already, hitting the one unsalted patch on them last winter when I'd come to get forms signed. Thank goodness it hadn't been with baked goods. That would have been messy.

I knocked on the window of Courtney's office, making her jump, but I needed her help with the main door.

"Sorry! I had been on the lookout for you," she said as she held the open the door for me. "And then I got a phone call, and the distraction was just enough for me to get caught up in other things once I hung up."

"No worries at all. Besides—" I gave her my cheesiest grin "—it's fun scaring you sometimes."

She led me into her office, patting a table by the window as she passed. "Right here's good."

I placed the boxes of cookies on the table. "Hope the committee likes them."

"Have you met the members on the town event committee? They *live* for the holidays. They'll be thrilled with cookies."

I pointed out the window. "Are they responsible for the gathering of gnomes outside? Or maybe it's a grouping. What do you call a bunch of gnomes altogether like that?"

She belted out a laugh. "Gnomie homies?" Still

chuckling slightly, she answered, "No. They were here this morning before the building was even open."

"So who did it?" I plopped into the chair across the desk from hers.

She lowered herself into hers. "Truthfully, I have no idea. It's not the first time they've been around. Did you not see them around this time last year?" When I shook my head, she replied, "They kept springing up in random places."

"So kind of like the football team flocking players' homes with flamingos?" It had been Alex's idea for a team-building activity at the start of football season.

"Kind of, but that at least includes a sign to say who did it, and there was some sort of rationale as to who moved it, how, and when. There were pictures and every-thing. This? No idea how the places get picked. Part of me thinks people just take a few from the various displays to go put them elsewhere or add to *gnomings* that are already somewhere. I've never seen so many at once. They were really popular a few years ago, so people might be trying to find something to do with them now. It's cute, though."

Nodding, I peeked out the window once more, curious if the ghosts I saw in town could be getting into the holiday spirit by moving them. "There is a sort of charm to them. Not your standard garden gnome statue."

"So now that you're here, and the cookies are here, I have one question for you." She folded her hands together on the desk. "What do you want for lunch?"

We grabbed lunch at Leafs and Grounds. The local

coffee shop was one of our favorite places. And going together meant we could split a sandwich and each get a cup of soup. To save time, we called our order in and drove down in her car, but only after Courtney swore—not for the first time—that my bike would be safe. There was no good spot to lock it to at Town Hall, and despite everyone in town's assurance that I didn't need to lock my bike, my car, or my apartment, years of living in a college dorm and in a city apartment had drilled locking my things up for security's sake into my head.

True to her word, the bike was right where I left it when we got back. However, something had changed.

"Oh my gosh. Would you look at that!" Courtney's voice held a hint of wonder.

I glanced up from my marshmallow rice treat, my one addiction in life. I'd grown up making the easy sweet, but they were Gary's specialty at Leafs and Grounds and I couldn't replicate it, not that I'd sell them if I could. First, I wasn't going to compete with Gary, and second, I wanted them all to myself. But since for whatever reason I couldn't make them quite as good, I settled for regular visits to the coffee shop.

I stopped in my tracks as I took in the sight. Surrounding my bike and trailer were at least half of the gnomes that had been on the front lawn of Town Hall. Two were in my empty trailer.

"What in the world?"

Courtney dissolved into a fit of laughter. "That is a good one. It had to have been someone who saw us leave together. I wonder if Brenna noticed anything. Her window is right there." She pointed directly above my bike.

Brenna wouldn't have seen anything if ghosts were responsible, though. I picked up one of the plush statues. They were squishier than I expected but heavier. Almost as if they were weighted at the bottom. "They are rather cute."

"You should take some back with you. I bet you could fit a bunch in the trailer."

"No, I couldn't do that." I lifted another gnome. "Besides, then everyone would see me moving them, and soon enough all of Heartwood Hollow would be saying that I'd been responsible for them randomly showing up places all this time."

"But you've only lived here a year. This has been going on longer than that."

I gave her a look as I tried to put another gnome under my arm. I had to at least clear a path for my bike.

She put her hands up in surrender before grabbing a couple gnomes to help me. "You have a point. This town does get a bit carried away with its rumors." Courtney had never addressed what the town had been saying about me. She didn't seem to care about all that. The rumor mill didn't interest her. Working in the mayor's office probably meant that she heard enough and had to keep a certain air of professionalism about her. Wouldn't do the town good if the mayor's assistant was causing drama. Courtney was likely aware of them, though. I didn't know how she couldn't be. Donna telling me about the rumors yesterday morning hadn't been the first time I'd heard them. They started soon after I arrived. Sarah had said it was because I was new. My arrival finally gave them all something different to talk about. But a year later, the rumors still hadn't died down. Instead, they'd multiplied. But it sold muffins and cookies, so until a time came when they started to hurt business, I'd let them be.

Together, Courtney and I moved all the gnomes back to the front lawn, and I pedaled away, shaking my head at thought of a group of Christmas gnomes guarding my bike. The gnomie homies were cute, and I wondered who was behind moving them all, or if it was like Courtney said, that multiple people were involved, almost giving them a life of their own as they traversed Heartwood Hollow.

CHAPTER 5

The gnomes had moved again by the next day. I saw some as I passed Cheese Louise on my way to the bakery. It was Tuesday, and the shop was closed, but I needed to stop by to measure my windows for the display. I would have done it yesterday, but once again Sarah had to shoo me out the door so I could get to another open house.

No luck with that one either.

I'd made window displays before, including one for Halloween, but I hadn't needed to be as precise with the decorations as much of it was draping black fabric and stringing fake spiderwebs over my selection of holiday-themed treats. Once again, I'd been thinking about those longer than anything else, and although I won "Best New Business Display," a category I believed only I was competing in, Sarah said I had to up my game for Christmas. No pressure. Several businesses in town were closed on Mondays, one reason why I chose to have Tuesdays and Wednesdays off so people on Main Street would always be able to find something open, but it seemed that many had taken the day off to decorate their windows. Some displays were complete, already out on display for all to see. Others were hidden behind large boards, building drama and suspense for the big reveal on Saturday.

Once I had the window dimensions, I quickly stopped into Leafs and Grounds for a marshmallow rice treat and a Sugar Plum tea. The wintery blend sounded too good to pass up. I let it sit in the car as I drove to the hardware store on the edge of town to grab some boards —not to cover my windows—and paint. If I was running with the idea of cookies for Santa, then I was going to make it better than anyone expected it to be.

Two homes on my way out of town had been gnomed. Of the three places I'd seen this morning with gnomes in front of them, none had as many as Town Hall had, but altogether, it seemed like there were more than I'd seen yesterday.

My tea had cooled down substantially by the time I'd gotten out of the hardware store. Although it barely could be called warm, I didn't mind. I preferred everything I ate or drank to be not too hot. The last thing I wanted to do as someone who worked with food for a living was to burn my taste buds. That wouldn't do me any good, especially right now as I tried my new recipes.

I dropped everything off at the bakery. Lacking space in my apartment meant I'd be doing most of the work there, including the painting. It was yet another reason why I wanted to find a house. I'd have the space to do prep work there. Then I could cart it to the bakery for a surprise finish.

The next stop on my list was the general store, across the street and only a few storefronts down from the bakery. It was one of the largest stores on Main Street and had a random assortment of things that catered to residents and tourists alike. It didn't make sense to go anywhere else until after checking there for all the decorations I needed for this display.

I stayed in the store for longer than planned as I had to listen to the big talk of the town. Something else had been stolen overnight. This time it was a pile of books next to a statue of a girl reading on a bench outside the library. The brass statue of the girl had been unharmed, but the books, which had been stacked and then coated in some sort of an all-weather protectant so that they always sat in statuesque ready-to-read condition for the little girl, were missing. They'd never been secured to the bench and had been moved dozens of times in my year here as people—mostly tourists—sat next to the girl to take pictures with her. Now the books were missing completely with no clues as to where they could have gone.

"What random things to have disappear throughout town," a woman in the aisle next to mine said to the clerk restocking the Christmas lights. "Sal's apron, Stay, and now the library books."

"Don't forget Sal's hat."

"Oh, but that goes missing regularly. Half the time I think it blows off his head."

Standing on tiptoes, I peeked over the shelves to see the two talking.

"There was that birdhouse from the pet supplies store that went missing," the clerk added.

"That was last year, wasn't it?" the woman shopping asked. *Shopping* may not have been the right word anymore. I doubted she'd moved for several minutes now.

The clerk shrugged. "Still, seems awfully similar to this."

"They never did find it, did they?"

The clerk shook her head. "Year before that, it was the old school bell from outside the historical society."

"You surely don't think that's related, do you?"

The clerk shrugged once more. "Who knows. They found that, though. Just odd is all."

The shopper sighed. "Well, I should let you get back to work. I have to go meet my mother for lunch."

"Oh yeah? How's she doing?"

I resumed my shopping at that point, not needing to continue listening to the woman's personal stories. Had it not been for the missing books catching my attention, I would have continued on my way several minutes before. I didn't like gossip and tried to avoid it as much as possible. It didn't feel right talking about people like that. Maybe it stemmed from my worry in school that my ex-best-friend, Ginny, would one day spill my secret and tell everyone I saw ghosts. The last thing I'd wanted was to be the center of the gossip circles back in high school. It was hard enough just getting through high school on a normal day, never mind had there been rumors about me claiming to see ghosts. Now, as long as the rumors stayed what they were and didn't harm business, I didn't mind finding myself the subject of them.

When I could no longer hear the two talking, I swung into that aisle. In addition to Christmas lights, it also contained all of the seasonal gift-wrapping options, and I needed some of that for my display. I couldn't have Santa coming to deliver presents without having presents. The clerk was still in the aisle stocking the shelves, but beyond a brief hello and her asking me if I needed any help, we didn't talk. Truthfully, she'd already helped me with the information her earlier conversation had provided.

After wandering the rest of the store, I headed to the checkout, grabbing a newspaper on my way so I could check the real estate listings over lunch. I walked out with nearly everything I thought the window would require, right down to a cheap Santa suit and a pair of black rain boots that I could put fake buckles on to make a bit more Santa-like. I'd probably gone overboard, but I could save much of this for later years as long as I could fit it all somewhere.

The bakery reminded me of how it looked in the middle of construction after I dropped off all of my new supplies. Dealing with construction was one thing I did not want to repeat anytime soon. It was one reason why I was being so picky with the houses I was looking at. I wanted one that wouldn't need work right away.

Despite my protesting stomach, I gave my plywood a coat of paint before leaving the shop. I could give a second coat if needed first thing when I got back. Once that was done, I headed home for lunch and to give Saffy a treat. She was used to me being home on my days off, reading with a cup of tea beside me and her curled up at my feet, but with so much to do to prep the windows, that wasn't happening today and wouldn't tomorrow either.

I might have overestimated my capabilities to pull this off in only two days.

CHAPTER 6

I clapped my hands together in a wiping fashion to free them from bits of paper that I'd hole punched to create snow. I'd considered getting some form of cotton batting from the general store, but they only sold it in big rolls, and I didn't need that much. Just enough to make it look like Santa had tracked some in while delivering presents. It wasn't like I was trying to make pillows or anything like that. Stepping back from my work, I took in the sight. Santa had been stuffed full of newspaper—including today's after the real estate listings yielded nothing new—and other packing supplies I'd hopefully be using soon. Now Santa was suspended a foot off the ground from my newly created chimney that I'd bribed Alex to come help me build after dinner last night. I had to apply a bit more paint to it once it was in place, but they were finishing details. The whole window had been transformed into a by the chimney scene with a hearth full of small branches and sticks that Steph collected for me during one of her walks through Riverview Park yesterday.

Steph loved going for walks. If she wasn't home or at work, Steph was somewhere outside no matter the weather. Both she and Alex spent more time outside than any of my other friends here. I'd noticed that many people here in town were like that. Sure, some complained about the cold, like Sarah, but others seemed to take it in stride. Perhaps that was because it wasn't uncommon to get snow into late April. I'd only been here a year, and even I knew about the snow-filled prom from ten years ago. The same freak storm had hit Sunny Valley a couple hours before it reached here, giving me a snow day from school.

In the other window sat piles of gift-wrapped boxes arranged around nearly my entire supply of cake stands. A couple had my regular display cakes on them—I didn't have the space to move them somewhere else for the season—but others were empty, waiting for cookies that I'd put there in the coming days. I'd add some each day until the stands were overflowing.

My favorite part of the display was in the Santa window. Santa's hand hung outstretched from underneath the chimney's opening onto the hearth, reaching for one last cookie before he left. I planned to hang a cookie midair using fishing line I'd bought at the general store. I hoped that the line would be invisible to most passersby and that the cookie would look as if it were floating to Santa using a little Christmas magic.

"Well, that is as good as it's going to get right now," I

said to an empty bakery. "I can touch up a few more things this afternoon once it all settles and dries."

The bakery lights took on a warmer tone for a moment as if a surge had run through them. I looked up at them, my lips pursed to the side. This was the third time in the last few days. I didn't want to have to call an electrician to come out again only for them to say nothing was wrong. Maybe a tenant upstairs was doing something to cause it or, if not that, had experienced something similar. I'd have to ask the next time I ran into one of them. Perhaps there wasn't something wrong with my bakery specifically. Maybe it was the whole building.

Or talk about a little Christmas magic, maybe the bakery liked my display. I chuckled. Wouldn't that be something?

The kitchen felt so empty as I entered it from the shop and flipped on the lights. It was weird being here without my team, but I could handle making Libby's cookies without them. I quickly made the base sugar and chocolate doughs. She'd get a mix of what she had on Sunday as well as a few of the varieties we'd made Monday. I hoped they would impress her like they had on Sunday. We had plenty of other inns and bed and breakfasts in town, but Riverview Inn was the one that made it as the cover photos of any articles that talked about where to stay when one was planning a trip here. Its picturesque views of Mill River couldn't be beat.

As the several kinds of cookies baked—I'd nearly fit all of them in at once—I cleaned up my workstation. While they cooled, I cleaned up what I could of the shop, sweeping up the bits of wrapping paper and wads of tape from it getting stuck to itself as I wrapped pastry box after pastry box. At least I'd have several already made once the season was over. It was a shame I didn't have a place to store them already wrapped. I'd likely have to do it all again next year depending on my theme. It was one more reason I wanted to move. Storage space. I had a basement here, which I'd paid a hefty sum to have cleaned and refrigeration installed so I could have as much space in the kitchen as possible for working. There was still some room in the basement, but I didn't want to clutter it with decorations. Especially when I preferred to keep it available to use as the bakery grew. Upstairs, I had a small closet that opened up into the kitchen, but it was already full with our coats and everyday decorations, not to mention a few things leftover from Halloween that I could see reusing.

Once the cookies had sufficiently cooled, I boxed them up to take to the inn. Even though I had my car here, I loaded up my bike trailer with the cookies. It was a few degrees warmer today than yesterday, the sun was shining, and I needed to take advantage of the remaining nice days of the year before the snowy season hit, making my car a necessity for deliveries.

The gnomes at the entrance to the inn were impossible to miss as I turned onto the long driveway for the grand bed and breakfast. I doubted Libby had put them there. They seemed too random in that spot, and she would have better incorporated them with the décor that was just now coming into view. The grand yellow home stood out brightly on the landscape that had started to turn its winter shades of beige and brown. A few of the maple trees running along the perimeter of the driveway still hung on to the occasional leaf, but the lawn had gone dormant, and the inn's beautiful garden where Libby got all of her flowers had been cut back. Now holly wound around the tall columns on the front porch, and a giant wreath with a large red bow hung from the main door.

I coasted to a stop outside the side door to the kitchen, then hopped off my bike. Libby must have been looking out the window waiting for me because she had opened the door within seconds of my reaching into the trailer to grab the boxes for her.

"Thank goodness you're here," she said as I walked inside.

The kitchen was a mess. It wasn't anywhere close to looking like this when I dropped off the cookies on Sunday. I hadn't known Libby long, but I'd gone to her teas on Wednesdays several times now, and this wasn't how she seemed to usually run her business.

I set the two boxes of cookies down on the table. "Is everything okay?"

"If I'm being honest, no, not quite." She picked up a butter knife, then used it to spread cream cheese across a slice of bread. One from a loaf of bread baked at the Corner Bakery from the looks of it. The bakery at the opposite end of Main Street had nearly thrown a wrench in my plans to open here in Heartwood Hollow. Fortunately, Zeke, the owner, didn't bake sweets.

"One of my large planter urns was stolen, evergreen branches that had been inside it and all," Libby continued. "So this morning I had to deal with the police regarding that matter. I can't really have them coming out here and my guests assuming the worst, so I took pictures and drove to the station."

I must have been so focused on the gnomes that I hadn't noticed the urn's absence, surprising given its size. "Oh, Libby, that's awful. I'm sorry to hear that."

"Heavens know how someone managed to lift it, never mind get it off the property. It weighs at least a few hundred pounds."

"Do the police have any leads?"

She shook her head as she slathered cream cheese onto another piece of bread. "No. And I just don't see anyone in town doing something like that." She sighed. "But it's going to be noticeable if anyone tried to put it somewhere in town."

"Well, several other things have gone missing throughout town, stolen actually."

"The police mentioned that." She pushed the plate of cream-cheese-covered bread aside as she placed a cucumber that had been next to her onto a cutting board. "I'm here so often that I don't always hear the latest news. Poor Clara, she loves that dog."

"Libby, would you like any help?" I was already taking off my coat. "You look like you could use a hand."

"I couldn't ask you to do that." She quickly cut the cucumber into coins.

With nowhere else to put it, I let my coat drop to the floor. "I don't mind, and I know guests will be arriving for tea soon. Let me at least put the cookies on the trays."

She grabbed a second cucumber. "You know what? Yes. Thank you."

We worked quietly for the next half hour as Libby continued to prep sandwiches and I loaded on cookies and then scones that Libby had made. The shop windows weren't going anywhere.

"Thank you again for your help," Libby said as she started loading finger sandwiches onto the trays. "I hope I didn't ruin your plans for the day, especially after making you come in to help me by making these cookies in the first place. They look lovely, and I appreciate that you have a few new kinds in here."

"Don't worry about it." I popped an end flap of one of the bakery boxes out of its slot to break it down. "The window decorating is going well, and I had to let some paint dry anyway. It will be good to go when I get back." It wasn't like anything in the shop could get up and leave.

I stood at the edge of the sidewalk staring at the windows to Suncraft Bakery. The one window with the gifts was mostly done. It needed more cookies, but I'd continue to put a few on each day to give people walking by a hint of what was to come. However, despite Santa and the chimney, the other window still looked a bit empty. Maybe another few gift-wrapped boxes would do the trick. I'd ask the team what they thought tomorrow.

After a making sure everything in the kitchen and shop was picked up and put away, I hopped in my car.

Although I didn't have anything scheduled with the realtor today, I figured it couldn't hurt to take a spin through the area, to see if there was anything new on the market. In all the window decorating hubbub, I hadn't looked at the listings today.

I drove to Bug Creek a few miles away, then worked my way back to the center of town, slowly going up and down streets. After an hour, the only new signs I'd seen were for Clara's dog missing statue.

Several clusters of gnomes had appeared at various houses too. I wondered if there was a particular reason for them to be at any one home or if it was random. I certainly didn't see a pattern, and everything Courtney had said made it seem as if there was no explanation for it other than someone took them and moved them.

At one, I assumed a realtor had moved them to try to get the house more visibility. The gnomes lined the sidewalk at the front of the house, a *For Sale* sign in the middle of the lineup. At another, it looked as if the house's owners had incorporated them into their decorations, which included several regular-looking garden gnomes and others that sported the logos of their favorite teams. I didn't recognize them, but then again, I wasn't a huge sports buff. I sold sports-themed cookies in the shop but stuck to either the colors of the Heartwood Hollow Hellcats or Howlers—the high school and junior high mascots, respectively—or general imagery like baseballs or other sports equipment.

I slowed as I came upon the largest grouping of gnomes I'd seen outside of Town Hall. The house sat on the corner with a porch at the front. Two floors and at least two rooms wide. A picture window overlooked the porch. From what I could see, no curtains hung in that window or any other. Did that mean it was empty? As I turned the corner, taking in the side of the fenced-in back yard, I resolved to call my realtor once I got to the apartment building.

"Hey, Kathy, it's Joanie Sunevall."

"Joanie," Kathy chimed, a cacophony of kid noise and music in the background. "How are you? We didn't have anything scheduled for today, did we?"

"No, no. Nothing scheduled."

She let out a small sigh of relief. "Oh good. I'm at the first of many afterschool holiday events, and I would have sworn I left this day clear."

"Oh, I'm sorry, I can let you go."

I envisioned her holding up a hand to stop me as she said, "It's fine. Like I said, the first of *many*. Let me just step out for a second." The background noise decreased significantly. "What's up?"

"I'm calling because I was driving around the neigh-borhood just in case like you told me too. There's this house on Phinney, and it looks empty. I'm wondering what you might know about it."

"Hmm . . . Phinney? Nothing springs to mind, but I'll check the MLS database tonight when I get home and call you. Maybe it's coming soon. I'll text a few people to see if they know."

"That would be great, thank you."

The noise grew momentarily louder before quieting again. Kathy muttered something, but it was muffled, not directed to me. "All right, Joanie. I have to let you go, but I'll talk to you soon."

I thanked her, and we hung up, allowing me to climb upstairs to my apartment, crossing my fingers that Kathy would have good news for me later.

CHAPTER 7

"Windows look good," Sarah said the next morning as she hurried into the kitchen, her bulky coat already slung over her arm. She pulled in a wave of cold air behind her. The temps had dropped significantly overnight.

I wiped my hands on my apron. "Thanks."

She hung up her coat, then made her way to the oven, where she stood for several moments, her back to it and her hands hovering a couple inches from the door. "I wouldn't be surprised if we end up with snow for the weekend."

"Nothing before Sunday," Bryan said. "Air's still too dry."

She raised an eyebrow at him but said nothing.

"Wouldn't it make a mess of the parade if it were to snow before then?" I asked.

Gina laughed. "Half of them can be pulled by sleds, I'm sure. Pickups could handle the rest."

"Stick around long enough and you'll see it a time or two," Bryan added.

"Oh, I'm staying. I'm trying to buy a house, remember?" I wasn't going anywhere. From the moment I stepped foot in town, this was the place for me. I came up next to Sarah to grab a tray of cookies ready for the case. "See you out there once you're warmed up."

"I'm coming, I'm coming." Sarah scooted around me and grabbed a tray, then followed me out into the shop.

I slid one of the cases open. "What do you think of the windows? For real, this time."

She set her tray on top of the case next to mine. "I like it. You're planning on adding more cookies over there, right?" She pointed to the far window with all the half-empty cake stands.

"Most definitely. But is this too empty?" I waved my hand in the general area of just beside the chimney, then explained my idea about the floating cookie. "It doesn't seem like enough, but I'm at a loss."

She shrugged. "I can see what you mean, but I'm not sure what to do either. But at least you still have a couple days to figure it out."

"Yeah," I said, walking back into the kitchen for another tray, "if you count today."

I picked up lunch for Sarah and me after a delivery to the portrait studio off Main Street where the photographer, Whitney, was doing some holiday-themed mini-sessions. She'd asked me to bring a "heaping supply" of cookies. The sets for the photoshoots included everything from cookie smashes—which explained the cookies—to sitting in boxes that looked like presents to riding in a sleigh made to look like it was in the snow. The backdrop featured some of the open fields around Heartwood Hollow covered in a blanket of white, likely the only snow anyone would be seeing for a while.

Despite the continued lack of snow, it was too cold to sit outside and eat. We didn't have chairs in the bakery, something I hoped to rectify someday, so standing at the back counter to eat was our only option.

"What do you know of the gnomes that seem to be here, there, and everywhere around town?" I asked before taking a bite of my panini.

"The *tomtes*?"

"Is that what they're called?"

She chuckled. "Well, they certainly aren't garden gnomes. Why?"

"They're just all over town, that's all."

In much the same fashion, she explained them to me like Courtney did, providing no hint at who had started this movement but agreeing that it was likely multiple people now. But Sarah didn't know there were ghosts in town who could have been behind it. Something didn't feel right about that theory, though. With as many tomtes as there were, a lot of ghosts would have had to been involved, and that wasn't typical ghost behavior. I couldn't tell Sarah that, however, but she did confirm that whoever was responsible only put them out at Christmas.

"I used to have one myself," she admitted.

"Used to?"

She nodded as she chomped a chip, her gaze toward the ceiling as she tried to look innocent. "One of the ones you've seen around town *may* just be mine. I couldn't resist."

"Do you know much about them?" I blew on my chai tea to cool it down some more. "Their origin, I mean."

"They're traditionally a Christmas decoration, and tomte is their Swedish name. They go by other names throughout the region, but I don't know what. The one I bought had come with a tag on its history." She bit into her sandwich.

I thought about my childhood friend Ginny. Her family had Swedish roots, and I wondered if she was familiar with them. Not that I could ask her. She hadn't spoken to me in years. I thought of the *lussekater*, St. Lucia Day Buns, that I'd learned how to make from her grandmother. I hadn't made them in a few years, but St. Lucia's Day was coming, but the buns would probably be considered a little too savory for what I was allowed to make here. One day I'd ask for clarification from the town council or even find out Zeke at the Corner Bakery if he minded my making them, but now wasn't the right time. Not while still in my first year of business. I'd wait to be more established first. Plus, Zeke's gruff demeanor slightly intimidated me.

"Still in there, Joanie?" I shook the thoughts from my head as Sarah tapped hers with a finger. "You look like you got a little lost in there."

"Just thinking about a recipe I made a few times." I wondered if I could sweeten the lussekater a bit so I could sell it, or better yet, maybe a Swiss cookie that I could add to my holiday lineup. Maybe I could make them tomte shaped.

"You're doing it again," Sarah said before sipping on her hot chocolate.

"Sorry. Hey, has there been any news from Drew about the ring?" Between looking for houses, the tomtes, things being stolen throughout town, and the buildup to the holiday, Drew's ring had slipped from the forefront of my thoughts. We hadn't found it cleaning the bakery, and he'd been disappointed but unsurprised when Sarah called to give him the update at closing the other day.

She was quiet as she swallowed a mouthful of sandwich. "Nothing that I've heard."

"Which means he hasn't found it." I'd only known Sarah a little over a year, but she was a huge gossip. Always knew everything about everybody, it seemed. She was the one who had first told me about the rumors in town about the good luck cookies and muffins, which led some to think I was at least "part witch."

I just wish she would have told me before Halloween, but Sarah had said she wasn't sure how I'd feel about it. I absolutely would have played it up in the shop with the decorations. There was a competition then too, but I'd played it safe. Too safe. Oh well. There was always next year.

"Poor guy. I can't imagine losing something that one, meant so much, and two, cost that much. I was shocked the first time I heard how much someone should expect to spend on an engagement ring." Of course, having gotten a number of my friends together, I knew that amount varied widely from nothing monetarily but everything sentimentally with a family heirloom to several weeks' worth of pay.

Sarah balled up the paper her sandwich had been wrapped in. "Hopefully he'll find it in his washing machine or something."

"Don't he and Megan live together already? I wouldn't want her to find it and ruin the surprise."

She chuckled. "Then it would be a surprise for both of them."

After work, I headed down the street toward the library. Already one of my favorite places in town, I'd quickly become a regular as I borrowed books to supplement my small apartment bookcase. My love of books had come from my mom, the head librarian in my hometown. Reading was how I settled down for the evening, along with a cup of calming tea and my cat at my feet. Except today, I wasn't beelining for the fantasy section, not right away at least.

"Hey, Pete." I walked up to the circulation desk where the regular afternoon librarian was scanning in a stack of books. "Where can I find the cookbooks?"

He arched an eyebrow at me, but his smile was teasing. "Don't you have enough of your own?"

"Sure, I do," I said with a chuckle, "but I can't say I've done a whole lot of Swiss and Norse baking."

Now his playful look turned into one of genuine

curiosity. "Little early to be starting New Year's Resolutions on learning new things, isn't it?"

"Just looking for some inspiration. Sarah said that's where all the tomtes originate from."

He nodded his head once long and slow as if that explained everything. "Well then, I'm going to suggest you head to the children's section. Emily? Can you hear me?" After a moment of no response, he rang a circular silver call bell sitting at his desk. "I always call for her first, but the ding carries better through the stacks."

Another moment more and a girl a few years older than me approached the front desk pushing a metal rolling cart half full of books. Her eyes lit up as Pete smiled at her. "What do you need?" She glanced at me then, a shy smile on her face. "Hello, Joanie. How are you today?"

I replied with a quick hello, but then she turned her attention back to Pete as he said, "Joanie here would like to see the display we have in the children's section."

She pushed her glasses up her nose and nodded. "Can I take that stack of books for you too?"

He smiled at her again, and a bit of color bloomed on her cheeks. It was obvious how much she liked him, no knack for getting couples together necessary. "Thanks, Emily." He lifted several books off the stack and handed them to her, then grabbed the rest as she put the first group on the cart and passed those to her when she was ready.

"No problem. Follow me, Joanie." She turned around with her cart.

When we were several feet away, I glanced over my

shoulder. Pete was busy at the desk again. "I actually wanted to see the cookbooks, so if you could point me over there."

Emily shook her head, pausing our walk to put a book back where it belonged. She then righted a book on the shelf above it. "If Pete says you need to go to the kids' section, that's where you should go. He's a genius when it comes to this stuff. I'm learning so much from him."

"Oh yeah?"

We resumed walking. "I've been putting myself through library school. Only a couple more semesters and I'll have my master's. I was thrilled to get an internship here with Pete—and everyone else who works here too. I'd love to work here eventually. Then maybe I could move here and not have to commute from the city."

The city she referred to wasn't anything like Boston or Providence or even Portland. But Snowhaven was home to a state university as well as a couple private colleges, making it worlds bigger than Heartwood Hollow, which was home to two thousand people at most in winter.

"I didn't realize you didn't live here."

"I grew up in Knoll's Grove, so not far away, but far enough I didn't want to put up with commuting to school in the winter. So I moved down there for grad school."

As we turned a corner, I realized why Pete had suggested this section. Decorating the space were a dozen more tomtes, each with a different kids' book featuring the gnomish creatures.

"All right. I get it now."

The corner of her mouth turned upward. "Pete was right?"

"He gave me a good starting point at least." If I didn't find some inspiration here, then I'd wander around until I found the cookbooks. It would probably be smart of me to learn where they were anyway.

"Great!" she chimed. "I'll leave you to it, then." She walked off with her cart.

I turned back to the tomtes.

Not wanting to disturb the display that the librarians had created, I only studied the tomtes up close rather than picking them up individually to see how similar they were to the ones I'd seen firsthand at Town Hall. These were slightly shorter but looked semisolid, the way the others had with stuffed insides that were weighted down so they wouldn't fall over when they were left standing outside. From what I could tell, some of them had posable arms, and several were holding things like tiny presents and small bowls full of white stuff. It wasn't real food, of course, but it was something. As I finished looking at those, I perused the books the library was offering about them. All were illustrated kids' books, no surprise given where I was in the library. Some were set outside in the woods and had wild animals like foxes and rabbits on the cover. But many took place in small towns or at farms. One, in particular, showed two tomtes running away holding a bowl of oatmeal over their heads. That must have been what the white stuff was in the bowls the few were holding. I picked up the yellow book and began to read.

It wasn't oatmeal, but porridge. It seemed that tomtes loved buttery porridge, and it was custom to leave some out for the tomtes around the farm. Especially on Christmas Eve, much in the same manner one left cookies for Santa.

I had my idea.

CHAPTER 8

Friday morning, the tomtes had moved around once more. It was almost becoming a game to me on my short walk to the bakery to see where some would end up. Today several were in front of the cottage set up for Santa in Founder's Park, joining the one that I had seen through the window the first day it was standing.

Crews had been out here every day adding something new to Santa's cottage or in the park around it. It seemed the town event committee had finally given up on the chance that there would be snow in time for Santa's arrival tomorrow, and a various array of materials had been laid out on the ground leading up to the cottage to create a path cleared through the snow. There was nothing in the pathway itself, but to each side, the ground was covered in white. Candy cane solar lights had been staked through the material, likely both to help keep it down if the wind ever picked up and to light the path for those coming to see Santa in the evening.

No doubt there would be work around the site today,

although to me, the only things that appeared to be missing were Santa's sleigh, his giant bag of gifts that was so large it had to sit outside the cottage, and the constant line of kids. All of those things would arrive after the parade.

The tomtes out in front of the cottage didn't seem to be a part of the crew's plans, but I wondered if they would end up incorporated into the design. I'd grown fond of the stuffed decorations over the past few days, more so now that I'd read several children's stories about them.

I unlocked the front door of the bakery, then stepped inside, locking the door behind me. There were still a few hours before I needed it open. I'd taken to coming inside via the front since setting up the window display so I could add a few of the day-old cookies to the growing piles I had set up, not that there were very many day-old cookies. They'd been flying off the shelves in almost the same way that I'd planned to have the one cookie floating to Santa before he went up the chimney.

I'd gotten many compliments on the display so far, but they hadn't seen anything yet.

I placed the few cookies I could onto the cake stands in the window, then headed into the kitchen, taking off my coat and placing it in the closet after dropping my duffel bag on my workstation.

When Bryan and Gina both walked in a few minutes later, they eyed the bag.

"What do you have in there?" Gina asked, coming to take a closer look, not that she could see inside the black duffel that was still zipped closed, hiding my newest cookie. Or rather, the ingredients for what I hoped would be my newest cookie.

"We're all learning something new today, but first we need to crank out more than our usual amount of treats as well as the muffins we need for Double Aitch and Olde Templeton. Plus there's a special order for the business owners' event tonight that's going to require even more cookies." For the most part, it was going to be all cookies all day. Bryan and Gina had been putting in more time this week as we increased our load for the holiday. Today was no different. They'd likely be here until after lunchtime, especially with what I had planned.

I'd been looking forward to tonight's event since the invitation arrived. Besides the fact I rarely got a chance to dress up, this would give me an opportunity to talk with my fellow local business owners in a less professional environment. I had big ideas for the bakery that included all of Heartwood Hollow. Hopefully, with enough sweets, I could butter up the town's entrepreneurs to get them to collaborate with me on a few things.

To tease Gina and Bryan a little bit, I unzipped the bag and then pulled out the ingredients: oats, rice, sour cream, cream, and to make sure we'd have enough once our regular baking was done, some butter, sugar, and cinnamon.

Gina pursed her lips as she studied everything. After a moment, I moved it all out of my way so I could start working. The last thing I wanted was to tip something over and create a mess back here. I had no time for a deep clean of the kitchen if that happened, not without missing the event. When one was a small business owner, one learned to do everything, even the heavy cleaning.

"But we've made plenty of oatmeal cookies before. Some even this week," Gina finally said.

"Remember what she said a few days ago when she had us do all the plain batches of the sugar and chocolate cookies, to trust her? I bet this isn't any ordinary oatmeal cookie," Bryan said. "Besides, we've never done anything with rice."

I smiled at Bryan, grateful for his vote of confidence. "Exactly. And as for cookies today, oatmeal is on the list again, along with more peppermint, peanut butter blossoms, and well, you'll see." I passed out the recipe cards for the new cookies we'd be making today along with the list of what we were repeating.

Gina grabbed a large mixing bowl. "Muffins first, though, yes?"

"Absolutely. Let's get to it."

Once Sarah seemed situated in the shop for the morning and most of the day's baked goods were done, aside from what we'd need for tonight's event, Gina, Bryan, and I descended on my work station as I laid out the recipe. Each of us was taking on a different variation for one half batch before letting it cool and making another slightly different version. At the end, we'd taste test all six varieties to determine which one would be my special cookie. Some with different ratios of oats to rice, others with more or less sour cream, or none in one case. The only thing the same was the use of a lot of butter.

"So what started all of this, Joanie?" Gina asked as she set up her mise en place for her first batch, dishing out all of the ingredients she needed in their required amount so she would be able to bake from start to finish without having to run around to get supplies.

"The tomtes."

"The what?"

"You know, the gnomes outside everywhere," Bryan answered.

"They're rooted in Scandinavian folklore," I explained. "They do farmwork, and they're paid in porridge with a hefty amount of butter on top."

"I do think that's a lot of butter," Gina said, a smile growing across her face, "but I love butter, so that's fine by me."

"Most of the stories tie into Christmas," I continued, pouring ingredients into my own small bowls, "Some tales even say the tomtes and nisse, which is another name for them, carry around large sacks of gifts for kids like Santa does."

Bryan took the oats off Gina's workstation. "No wonder they became such popular Christmas decorations."

"There are more and more here every year. It's like we could be the sister city of wherever they first originated." Gina laughed. "At least at Christmastime."

We had a good chuckle over that, then quickly set out to work making our cookies. Within the next hour and a half, the six batches were baked and cooling. I called Sarah into the back.

She seemed a bit frazzled. "It's been hopping out there, I don't want to be away for long."

No one had been in there when I'd grabbed her, but I wouldn't keep her. "Okay, then take this one, and I'll be out with the rest labeled for you. I want your honest opinion on your favorite."

She nodded, taking the cookie with a fifty-fifty mixture of oats and rice out of my hand. I grabbed a plate for her and arranged the remaining five cookies like a clock. At the center of the dish, I put one of my recipe cards with arrows pointing to each and a quick note of what made them different from one another. I dashed into the shop and placed the plate on the back counter behind Sarah. She wasn't exaggerating about it being busy. There were three small groups in there who hadn't been moments before.

Gina and Bryan were politely waiting for me as I walked back into the kitchen. "Ready to try them?"

We each picked up a cookie and sunk our teeth into it, the same one Sarah had tried first. After each one, we cleansed our palates with sips of water and oyster crackers, then shared our opinions. By the end, there was a clear winner. Even Sarah agreed.

"Great! Then let's make a full batch of these for tonight's event, and then we'll make a double batch in the morning. I'll head to the store after work to make sure we have enough supplies. Rice isn't a common one for us, and I don't want to run out." I gathered the cookies from the non-winning batches and put a few on my workstation, then went to put the rest in the window display.

"I think that just about fills up those stands," Sarah said as I rearranged the cookies to highlight the varieties that the bakery had to offer. "Did you figure out what you're doing with the space in the other one?"

I wiped my hands on my apron, about to answer her, but a mother and her toddler walked in, and I didn't want to ruin the surprise for them. "You'll see," I said instead, heading back toward the kitchen.

Gina and Bryan had already started in on the next round of baking in the few minutes I'd been gone, cleaning off their workspaces and loading a rack to run through the dishwasher. I maneuvered around them, gathering supplies for my next experiment.

I set a saucepan on the stove and plopped a chunk of butter into it, then added a heaping of sugar. About a third of a cup. I rarely needed to measure things because I was able to eye my amounts almost exactly, be it a teaspoon or a half cup. I'd refined the skill over the years, but it had always come easily to me. Likely it was one of the reasons why my gram called me a kitchen witch. But then again, almost anything I did in the kitchen elicited that comment from her. Gram wasn't much of a cook. She could boil water for pasta and pota-toes, although she mainly used her stovetop to heat water for tea. Her oven stored the pots and pans she rarely used.

"So what are you making now?" Gina asked.

"Remember how I told you the tomtes' porridge always had to have butter on top or else they wouldn't be happy?" Seeing her nod, I continued, "I'm trying to find a way to do it in cookie form. Hopefully a sweet butter sauce will do the trick."

"Gotta give you some creativity points there," she said. "I wouldn't have thought of this. A tomte porridge cookie? That's great stuff."

"And that's why she's the bakery owner and we work for her," Bryan replied.

With the butter melting, I added in a little cream, then a little more, stirring occasionally. Once it looked good to me, having a smooth but viscous consistency, I placed one of the remaining cookies from the good batch on a plate. Using the spoon I'd been mixing with, I dropped some of the sauce onto the cookie's center and let it spread naturally the way one would if a pat of butter was placed on top of a dish and allowed to melt on its own.

I popped it into the refrigerator to let it set for a minute, then pulled it back out and broke it into quarters. Gina and Bryan ate theirs as I brought one into Sarah. Her eyes lit up as she tried it. "Okay, it was good before, but now it's perfect."

"Great, that's what I was hoping to hear." I dashed back into the kitchen, both to have my cookie and to get back to baking. There was still a lot to do before the business owners' event tonight.

<h1 style="text-align:center">CHAPTER 9</h1>

"What do you think?" I held the green dress up to my body and stood facing the mirror. "I like it. The color's good."

I watched for my calico cat's answer in the reflection. She sat on the middle of my bed, eyes half shut, her tail slowly flicking back and forth.

"Don't look at me like that, Saffy. I can't stay tonight. I'll only be gone for a few hours."

Saffy's eyes widened and she flopped to her side, exposing her belly and trying to be cute. Little did she know, she was cute even when she wasn't trying. I gave her belly a quick scratch but pulled my hand away before she could decide I'd given the spot too much attention.

"You know I have to go to this. It will be good for the bakery." And me. I was having a conversation with my cat. Again. "And you're getting dinner before I go."

At the mention of dinner, she rolled onto her feet,

then hopped off the bed, no doubt to go wait by her bowl.

I got myself dressed, pulling my hair half up and letting the rest flare out at my shoulders. My usual pony-tail style wouldn't work for my outfit or the event. I wasn't going anywhere super fancy, but the large dining room at the inn deserved more than my regular winter apparel.

Turning around in front of the mirror, trying to give myself a three-sixty view, I declared myself good to go. But before I could, I had to keep a promise to my cat.

Like I thought, Saffy was sitting by her bowls, tapping the empty food dish, clearly impatient with me. "Don't worry, I didn't forget about you," I told her as I grabbed the silver bowls and placed them in the sink.

She eyed me with skepticism as I opened the cupboard.

"You have other bowls, you know." Shaking my head slowly, I pulled out a second set, then put them on the counter. When she saw her dry food come out of the corner next, her ears perked up. I poured some into one bowl, and she backed up a half step to let me put it in front of her. She did a whole body wiggle, ending with the rapid shaking of her tail as she stuck her face in the bowl. A happy *purt*—a cross between a purr and a chirp —escaped in between bites. I filled the second bowl with fresh water, then put it down next to the first.

After a few minutes, I scooped a spoonful of canned food on top of what she was eating, then popped a reusable lid on the can before slipping it into the fridge.

"All right, I'm going to head out. I'll see you later, but don't wait up."

She didn't answer. She rarely did when eating. Not that she could verbally, although I wouldn't have been surprised given the way she looked at me sometimes. Saffy had strong opinions, and even though she couldn't talk, she found many ways to express them.

After putting on my heavier winter coat, I slung my purse over my head and then grabbed my nice shoes. With the lack of snow, I wasn't worried about ruining them, but I wasn't taking any chances in wearing heels longer than I had to. Besides, driving my station wagon was much more comfortable in sneakers. Kept my feet warmer too.

The drive to the inn took only a couple minutes. The walk from the inn's parking lot and up to the front of the house took longer. The foyer had a giant Christmas tree in front of the staircase. Even though I had come to the tree trimming on Wednesday evening and saw the tree then, I still marveled at the stunning sight. The ornaments ranged in size from eight or nine inches in diameter at the bottom to two or three at the top in various colors. Many seemed to have hand-painted scenes on them or were handcrafted with fabrics, ribbons, and beads. Some of the scenes I recognized. One had the old Dunmore Mill and waterwheel, another featured Town Hall. Others of Main Street or a view of the river from somewhere in Riverview Park. Prominently displayed was one depicting the inn itself.

"Beautiful, isn't it?" a familiar voice asked. "Every

year I go with a different theme. This year it's round ornaments."

"I was going to say I didn't remember them from last year." I turned toward Libby. She was beautiful in a long midnight-blue dress with rhinestone accents made to look like snowflakes. It almost looked like she could call down the snow if she desired.

"Last year was carved wooden ornaments. We had to rig a lot of them in unique ways to get them to sit just right." She opened her arms up wide and pulled me in for a hug.

It was warm and comfortable with the perfect amount of squeeze. "Merry Christmas, Joanie. Come, let's go take care of this coat."

She led me to the office to the side of the entryway across from the parlor where she held her teas. Inside, several rolling garment racks had been set up.

I pulled off my coat. "Do you have any guests staying with you tonight?"

"Oh, yes," she replied, passing me a hanger, "but they're already checked in and either up in their rooms or out enjoying the town. Billy will be on call tonight so that I can enjoy myself. Have you met my husband yet?"

"I actually have not met the mysterious Billy yet." I arranged my coat on the hanger, then put it back onto the rack.

She laughed. "He's not all that mysterious, I assure you. More he's not into small talk, but I'll make sure to introduce you when he makes his appearance tonight." She took my arm, spinning me back out toward the entryway, then led me down to the formal dining room. "Your cookies are here. Bryan dropped them off earlier. I like him. Dependable fellow."

I nodded. "He is that."

We turned into the dining room. The tables, overflowing with food, had been pushed toward the walls, chairs set up in strategic locations, and the usual cream curtains swapped out for red and green. The overhead lights had been dimmed, and the sconces on the walls provided additional light.

"Please tell me you didn't prep all this," I said.

"Everything that wasn't brought in from a local business to eat was catered by the same people who are tending the bar." She swept her arm up in a displaying fashion to show two younger gentlemen in white shirts and black ties behind a bar in the corner of the room. She broke out into a grin. "They even clean up."

"That sounds like a good deal to me."

"Oh, it is. Well, I need to go back to the entry to welcome anyone else who arrives. Most know their way down here, but what sort of a host would I be if I wasn't there to greet people?" She patted me between the shoulders, then disappeared back down the hall.

I glanced around the room, hoping to catch a familiar eye, but I didn't know many of the people who were here yet. So I headed over to the food, hoping to strike up a conversation with anyone else grabbing something to eat.

There were several recognizable elements on the table. The garlic knots could only have come from Nick and Etta's, the Italian restaurant close to my bakery. The large pasta bake next to them had probably been the contribution from Salvatore's. Further down were chicken quarters, my guess from the barbeque place right on the town line, and the cheese plate was likely from Cheese Louise.

"You're not going to find them, in case you were looking."

I spun around to see Gary from Leafs and Grounds holding his own plate, and I knew immediately what he was talking about. A small frown appeared on my face. I loved those marshmallow rice treats.

"That doesn't mean they aren't here, though. They got relegated to desserts. The soup is mine too, though. They're passing it around in tiny cups."

As if by magic, a waiter carrying a silver tray full of tiny two-ounce ceramic mugs appeared behind us. "Soup shooter?" he asked, holding the tray at a slight angle.

I picked one up. "Don't mind if I do."

Gary politely held up his hand, refusing a cup. "I've had enough in the making of it."

"This is a cute little logo," I commented, noting the tall trees with interlocking *H*s in the center beneath a snowflake.

"It's this year's town holiday emblem. Every year there's a competition for it. Looks a lot better full color, but the mugs are cheaper if you only do one color. Many of us have a huge collection of them. Make good ornaments if that's your thing."

I blew across the mug.

"Shouldn't be too hot," Gary said, nodding to the cup.

"It's just hot enough since you're supposed to drink it all in one or two sips."

"Can't be too careful." I downed the soup, the minty flavor tingling my tongue. "Oh, this is good."

"You like? It's a peppermint ginger soup."

As he spoke, I felt the warmth from the ginger from out of nowhere. "A perfect finish. You have something good here."

"Thanks. I want to remind people that we're more than just coffee and tea. You come for lunch regularly, but how many others? I can't tell you the last time some of them have been to Leafs for more than their morning brew."

I nodded in understanding. Events like this were vital to us. "We have to be able to rely on one another to support each other's businesses and recommend them to town visitors."

He nodded. "We're not competition for one another. We need to lift as we climb, so to speak."

I could get behind that one hundred percent. It was why I was looking to partner with other businesses through town. "We're in it together."

"And on that note, how about we finish getting our food, and I'll introduce you to some people. You're still new, so I'm not sure who you know or not."

True to his word, Gary used his talkative coffeeshop charm and brought me around to the various groups, more and more forming as others arrived. I didn't get a good opportunity to strike up my proposals for partnering with anyone, but a few agreed to meet for coffee to chat more when I broached the subject.

After a while, I found myself in a group of six. Gary had excused himself to chat with some people from the beverage trail that ran through town, leaving me to make small talk with the others.

"So what do you do?" I asked them all.

Two, a husband and wife, ran a gift shop at the top of Main Street. A third ran the general store. The fourth was none other than Louise from Cheese Louise, and I gushed over her grilled cheeses and wished again that I could make savory foods. She'd make a great partner for various cheese breads. I quickly looked around. Zeke from the Corner Bakery was nowhere to be found. I wondered why. Although we'd technically been invited to the event tonight, it wasn't something one said *no* to. The invitation felt more like a nicety to a required appearance.

"I'm the owner of a cleaning crew," the fifth said in a slight accent. "Name's Xavier."

I held my free hand out toward him. "Nice to meet you."

"And you own the bakery, correct?" he asked, a shy smile on his face, as we shook hands.

"I do. Well, one of them. Suncraft Bakery opened this spring, although it's been mine for just over a year now. There was a lot to get done."

"Ah, so a little newer than my cleaning business."

"What got you started in that?"

"Family. They run a cleaning business in Knoll's Grove. I worked for them all through school but wanted to start my own company. As I'm sure you know, Knoll's Grove is just as small as this, so I wasn't going to try to compete with my family for clients. They never saw a reason to come out this way, so I saw an opening. Got myself a little apartment on Main Street here and a storage unit for all of my supplies. Just hired my second employee."

"That's wonderful. Well done. I hope to be adding to the bakery staff soon myself. This holiday season has shown the necessity of getting another person in there."

He nodded. "I bet it's a busy time for you."

"Even more than I expected."

We continued to chat for several minutes and really seemed to be hitting it off, in more than just a professional manner. He laughed easily and smiled easier. It was nice talking to him, and eventually the others in the group wandered away to let the two of us talk.

And then it happened.

I felt it.

The matchmaking tingle.

All my life, I'd been good at setting people up with the one they were meant to be with. Even as a kid. My babysitter married the guy I said she should ask out one day while we were at the playground. He'd been there with his little brother. That was the first time I'd felt it. The tingling started in my toes, and it got stronger as the couple neared, and finally it reached a crescendo when they met. Afterward, the tingling would ebb and flow, but it was always there when the matches were together. I could even figure out how things were going in their lives as a result of the strength of that vibration. It was a skill that ran in the family. My mom was able to do the same thing.

I looked up to see who had come through the door, wondering if possibly it could be one of the couples I'd gotten together since I'd moved here. There were three, so it was a possibility, for sure, in this tiny town. But it wasn't one of my matches.

At the entrance to the dining room stood Whitney from the photo studio, and as we made eye contact, she waved. I felt the tingle grow stronger as she came closer, and it led right to Xavier. So much for us hitting it off. This was why I never dated. How awkward would it be if I was on a date and I found out my date's match was our waitress? No, thank you. At least Xavier and I had just been talking.

Whitney greeted us with a dazzling smile.

"You look gorgeous," I told her. She was wearing a cream-colored sweater dress that hugged her form down to her knees. But not one to take herself too seriously, she had large dangly earrings in Christmas colors featuring Santa with a bag of presents on his sleigh on one side and several reindeer on the other.

A flush colored her face as she did a three-sixty, her gaze repeatedly darting back to Xavier. He was being polite, but I could tell he wanted to talk to her.

It was time to relieve them of their curiosity. "Whitney, have you met Xavier?"

She shook her head, her smile turning shy as she stuck out her hand.

His smile matched hers. He lifted her hand and brought it to his lips. "Lovely to meet you. Joanie was right, you know. You look beautiful tonight."

"Why, thank you." Her cheeks grew even redder.

"Whitney runs the photo studio in town," I said, hoping to give them a bit of a push or else they'd stand here staring at one another all night. But the push only needed to be a small one. Now that they were together, they'd be fine. Sometimes an introduction was all my matchmaking duties required. Sometimes it took a bit more convincing, but if the tingling feeling existed, they were meant to be.

"Oh wow." Xavier's eyes widened as he spoke. "I've always had an interest in photography. All of the nature here makes for a wonderful subject."

I placed my hand on Whitney's shoulder. "I'm going to go get something else to eat. It seems that I have left you both in good hands." I turned to Xavier. "It was nice to meet you. Good luck with your business enterprise."

"Oh, before you go"—he dug into his pocket, then produced a business card—"this is my information in case you ever require cleaning services."

"Thank you." I took the offered card, then slipped it into a pocket of my wristlet. "You both have a great rest of the evening."

The two had already resumed their conversation by the time I'd turned toward the food table. I wondered what the townspeople would think of me when they learned I had a hand in getting another couple together. It wouldn't take long for me to find out. Donna would probably tell me. Or Sarah.

I was almost to the food tables when the waiters began swapping out the dinner trays for dessert, and I quickly spotted the marshmallow rice treats. That and a cookie would turn this night around. Cookies made everything better.

"I hoped I'd run into you tonight," someone said from close behind me.

I immediately perked up at the voice, hope growing in my chest. "Do you have any news?"

CHAPTER 10

I turned to find my realtor, Kathy, a few feet behind me.

A large smile was already plastered to her face. "I do have news! That house is up on the market. Good eye. I already called to try to get you in, but they aren't showing it until Sunday."

"All right." I sighed, wishing I could have gotten into it first thing tomorrow.

She gave me an understanding look. "They didn't want to miss taking their kid to the parade and to see Santa."

"Oh my goodness, that's right." In the moment, I'd forgotten all about tomorrow being the kickoff to the major town festivities. Tonight was just a precursor, a fun night for those of us who were about to enter our busiest season of the year.

I nodded hard once. "Okay. I'll make it work with my team. What time?"

"There's an open house from one to three. Shall I meet you there?"

"How about right at one? I want to get in there as soon as possible and see it. I love the location and the porch."

She took a piece of paper out of her bag. "Here's a bit more of a write-up for you on the property. Size, sewers, that sort of thing. It will also tell you all about the electricity, too, when it was last updated and how much they paid last year. I put in a few extra calls. I know after what you've been dealing with in the bakery that it's been a concern of yours."

"Thanks." I appreciated her going the extra step. Her husband was the electrician who'd come to work on the bakery's wires when I first saw the lights brighten in the shop with no explanation. That was how I'd first met her. It just worked out she was a realtor too. Funny how that happened sometimes.

She smiled. "Okay, well I will see you again on Sunday. She admired the table. I'll let you get back to your food. Doesn't it all look delicious?" She reached for a cookie but then tapped one hand with the other as if scolding herself. "Told myself I need to finish making the rounds before I get dessert."

I had made no such deal with myself, and took two marshmallow rice treats, one of my cookies—I rarely had a chance to eat them at an event I was making them for—and a chocolate mousse in a plastic cup made to look like a wine glass. Then, needing to find somewhere to eat it all, I left the room, having seen tall round tables just outside. The hallway was brighter, lighter, and less noisy. It was just what I needed to recharge a bit. As much as I enjoyed interacting with people when they came into the bakery, I liked my alone time too.

I wasn't the only one hiding in plain sight, however. Libby was doing the same, having taken a chair that had been stacked up on top of others and set it down for her to sit in. Next to her in another chair was a man, who I assumed was her husband.

"Ah, well this makes finding you easy," Libby said with a chuckle. "Just resting my feet a bit before I go back in and socialize some more. This is my husband, Billy. Billy, this is Joanie, the baker in town."

He politely stood and offered a hand. "Nice to meet you. You make delicious cookies."

"Oh, thank you. You have a lovely home."

"Ah, that's all Libby. She's the reason everything looks as nice as it does." At that moment, something nearby beeped. Billy pulled a phone from his pants pocket. "That's room four. I should go take this. Sorry to run." He kissed Libby on her head. "Again, nice to meet you, Joanie." Then he darted away, pressing his phone screen as he brought it to his ear.

"He's got more of the business sense," Libby explained as we watched her husband's retreating form. "I'm the one with all the lofty dreams for this place ever since we bought it. You should have seen it. Vacant for years."

I swept my gaze in an arc from one end of the hallway to the other. "You must have put a lot of work in."

She nodded. "Still do. Which is why I was hoping to

catch you again tonight. Now, you don't have to say anything tonight, but I'd love it if you'd consider becoming my permanent baker for tea time. And I mean beyond just the holiday season. Having to deal with the stolen urn the other day . . . well, it made me glad you were already doing the baking for the tea, and I realized that one less thing on my plate permanently would be a good thing."

I said nothing, expecting her to continue. She was a talker from every interaction I'd ever had with her.

"Now, I'm still going to make the sandwiches. I know all about how you aren't able to make anything of that nature because of your agreement with the town council. It was big news that you were opening. Don't know a person who wouldn't be aware of it. So you don't need to worry about that, but I would love it if you would make the cookies and the scones. You do make scones, don't you?"

"I do."

She signed with relief. "Oh, good. I thought so. I remembered seeing them in your shop, but it was a while back, and for all I know, it could have been a special order or something. I don't get out much into the town, as you know. Part of what I'm hoping you can do for me with your baking. Free up some of my time so I can get out and reestablish some of my old connections."

"Well, Libby, I think you have yourself a deal."

Suddenly a look of horror crossed her face. "Oh, wait! You said you aren't open on Wednesdays. I can't ask you to do it on those days. That wouldn't be fair to you."

I held up my hand. "It's really no trouble, and I've been thinking that I could expand the bakery somehow after the holidays. This is one way to do it and earlier than I'd hoped too, which is great. So yes, I can do Wednesdays. I'll talk it over with my team. It will happen, even if it's just me doing them again like it was this week for a while." This was just what I needed to give Sarah another day at the shop.

"Oh, thank you, thank you, thank you!" She clasped her hands together and shook them in my direction.

"You know this means I'm not going to be able to come to your teas anymore, though, since I'll be working."

She frowned slightly. "Well, everyone needs a day or an afternoon off sometimes. I'm sure I'll see you again at the tea table soon. You could always just stay after your deliveries one day."

I smiled, knowing that it wasn't likely to happen as soon as she or I hoped. I didn't like to take time off, and I'd been doing it regularly lately. Just an hour here or an hour there as I met with my realtor, but I hadn't expected it would take this long to find a house. A few months now already. How much longer?

We chatted a little longer, allowing me to finish my desserts, but finally it was time to face the crowds once more.

"Come on, let me introduce you to a few people."

"I can't stay much longer. The bakery keeps me to early hours." That was the one thing I'd change about the bakery if I could. The hours were so early. If the world were perfect, I'd have made the hours be later, but so many people stopped at bakeries first thing in the morning that I'd based my hours on that. It worked out well, as I quickly got the two diners as regular muffin customers. I would never be able to justify not being open early.

"All right, well, there are just a few, some of the other inn and B&B owners. Who knows, maybe you can strike up a few business deals with them too."

CHAPTER 11

The next morning, the gnomes looked like they had all congregated at Santa's cottage as if they were lining up to see the parade. They'd take up every spare inch of space along the sidewalk. The row of them continued past the bakery and in front of the shop next to mine. Some sections were two deep with gnomes staggered between others as if looking over their shoulders so they could see the procession of floats and cars that would be happening in a few hours.

I opened the bakery door, then stepped inside and locked it behind. Pulling a decorative plate that I'd bought from home out of my bag, I walked to the window with the chimney. Christmas themed, of course, the plate was red with white snowflakes that looked like they were part of a sweater. There had been several ugly sweaters last night, including one ugly sweater dress. I'd have to incorporate the design on a cookie if they were that popular here.

After setting the plate down, I headed into the

kitchen. I flicked on the light in the kitchen and got started right away on the muffins. Bryan and Gina would be here soon. Both Olde Templeton and Double Aitch diners needed larger than usual orders because of the foot traffic that was expected on Main Street today. Many people set out chairs early, a way of saving their spots in the cold without having to be standing there until the time got closer. Then they'd get a coffee from Leafs and Grounds or would pick up a full breakfast from the diners or even stop in here for muffins that they could eat in a bag from their spots along the parade route.

It was a busy day, capped by the opening of the cottage that had been sitting next to the bakery all week. It was fully decorated now, and I couldn't wait to see it lit up with Santa inside. I'd been waiting for days and looking forward to the holiday season officially being on underway.

Bryan was the first to arrive and he immediately dived into helping with the muffins, taking over once I put my batch in the oven. Gina walked in only a few minutes behind him and got started on scones. We had a new variety today to go with the Christmas theme. Cherries and chocolate chips with a white chocolate drizzle. It was a play on Santa's suit.

I switched over to cookies. I needed to make sure I had at least one batch done and fully cooled by the time I got back from the morning deliveries so I could finish the last of the window display. I didn't know quite when the judges would be walking around to look at all the windows on Main Street, but the winner was part of what they announced when Santa arrived at the cottage.

He, of course, made the official announcement after the formal holiday greetings.

I had to be ready.

The tomte porridge cookies were only part of the design.

"I'll be right back," I told my two bakers once I returned from the morning's deliveries.

"But you just got back," Gina said, sliding a tray of cookies into the oven.

"This is official holiday window business, you won't even know I'm gone." In truth, it would only take me a minute to get what I needed before returning to the shop. I wanted this done before Sarah got here. It needed to wow her. I'd know from her reaction as soon as she saw it.

I grabbed a porridge cookie from the tray and headed out into the kitchen. The first thing I did was set it on a clear sheet of plexiglass. Alex had called in a favor with his buddy at the hardware shop to get me a circular piece cut that was about four inches around, just a bit smaller than my cookie. I wanted the cookie to cover it all. Somehow, Alex had rigged it to sit in a little bit of fishing line crossed under it like an X. Some sort of string hammock that wouldn't block the view of the cookie. If anything, maybe the string would look like it was sparkling if it caught the light.

I carefully moved the fishing line to get the cookie on the plexiglass, then rearranged the string to balance the entire contraption. I stood back, holding my breath as it tilted a little one way with a bit of a spin before settling. The slight tilt worked in my favor, displaying just a bit more of the cookie toward the window without it looking like it was hanging precariously. It also hid the plexi better. It was a win in my book.

My decorating work wasn't done, however. I stepped outside, instantly regretting the mistake of not grabbing my coat, and then rushed to the tomtes. After grabbing two that seemed to have moving arms, I darted back inside and put both in the window. Now I needed the central piece.

"Back! I said rushing into the kitchen before taking a tray of porridge cookies that had sufficiently cooled. Before anyone could reply, I was already back in the shop.

I placed the tray on the case nearest the window, then began arranging cookies on the ugly sweater plate. Once they were properly arranged, I set the plate on a clear glass cube riser.

With that set, I grabbed the first tomte.

"Hello again." Upon further inspection, I recognized him as one of the tomtes that had been in my bike trailer the other day at Town Hall. "Thank you for helping me this morning. I hope you enjoy the window." It dawned on me then that I was like all the rest in town who had been taking tomtes and leaving them elsewhere for the joy of others. That was what I hoped this window display would do. Bring joy. And maybe a win for me on the window decorating contest. That would be wonderful for my first year in business.

I set the tomte in the window on the right side of the plate, then adjusted his arms so it looked like he was supporting the plate with both hands. Then I did the same with the second tomte, put him on the left side. I hoped it looked like the two were running off with the plate to keep all the cookies for themselves as Santa tried to magically lift one into the air to grab a final bite on his way up the chimney. It was my play on the traditional story of the tomtes. I couldn't make porridge for them to take as payment for all their work, but I could make porridge cookies. With the buttercream poured onto each cookie as if it were melting butter on a bowl of porridge, I felt I'd achieved the look.

Now it was all up to the judges. Hopefully they had been to the library to see the display or otherwise knew of the stories. If they didn't, then I didn't know what I'd do. It might not look cohesive enough, just random pieces thrown together to take up space. Nothing I could do about it now.

"All set," I announced as I walked back into the kitchen and to my workstation. We'd need a lot more cookies, no doubt about that. And that was even with us being closed during the actual parade. All the shops shut down then since no one would be moving along the street until it was over. Plus, it gave us all the opportunity to enjoy the parade ourselves.

Although many breaking from work would probably stay in their shops to watch, I planned to experience all of it outside with everyone. I loved a good parade. And I wanted to hear the reactions of those around who settled in to watch the parade close to the windows. If the judges didn't understand it, the kids would. Since putting up Santa, I'd even worried a few that he wouldn't be able to go to the parade or even make it to their houses for Christmas if he was stuck in my fake chimney. I assured them all that Santa was fine and they'd see him in the

cottage real soon.

We just had to make it through the parade first.

Sarah burst through the kitchen door a few minutes earlier than she usually did.

"Oh my goodness, that looks so good!" she exclaimed as she crossed the room to hang up her coat. "I love how you have gotten into the town spirit with the tomtes."

"You think it will go over well?"

"Absolutely. Everyone loves those things. You didn't put them all outside in front here and in the park too, did you?"

I shook my head. "No way. That would have been a little ambitious given the hour I got home last night." I would have already been asleep by then had it been a normal night. Or at least reading, finishing up one last chapter.

"That's right! How did that go? Meet any of Heartwood Hollow's most eligible?"

"If you mean business partners, then, yes." If she wasn't talking about this, that, or the other rumor going on about me, then she was trying to set me up with someone. I assumed she did it because if I was matching people up, then I should try to find someone for me to be with. It didn't work like that, though. From what Mom had said, whatever it was that we could do didn't work on ourselves. Eventually Sarah would learn that wasn't in the cards for me. Xavier last night had proven once again why I didn't date.

"Well, I heard that you are partially responsible for one of my roommates having a wonderful evening thanks to you introducing her to someone."

"Again?" both Gina and Bryan said with varying degrees of surprise.

Sarah nodded emphatically as she grabbed a tray of cooled cookies from the rack, then as she headed back toward the shop, over her shoulder commented, "I hear they have a date tonight."

"I didn't realize you were roommates with Whitney," I replied as I followed her with a tray of my own.

"Her, me, and Jill. Friends since high school." She studied me a moment as she set her tray down. "It's early still, but this is going to be the fourth couple you've gotten together this year, isn't it?"

Trying to be non-committal about the answer, I shrugged and instead changed the topic. "So you really like the windows? Think I stand a chance?"

"You should ask the judges. They're on their way now."

CHAPTER 12

Sarah pointed out the window, then gave the panel of five a quick wave hello. They returned with smiles and waves of their own as they walked up close to the display, snapping pictures of details and then stepping back to take overall shots of each window.

I couldn't tell who the judges were. They were bundled up in their winter gear. Hats down over their ears, chins buried into their scarves, some with hoods over their heads. I assumed they were all from the town event committee, not that I knew who was a part of it. I needed to get out in the town more, meet more people. Maybe then I'd be able to tell who they were.

The judging was making me nervous. I felt a little as if I was in a fishbowl with the way they were staring in as Sarah and I loaded the cases.

As the judges stood outside, the Main Street area around them grew busier. Many seemed honed in on their destinations. Several people passed by and slowed to look at the bakery windows. And a family of four—a grandmother, parents, and a teenage son—set up chairs right behind the judges and sat, claiming their parade spot.

After several minutes, a judge knocked on the door.

Sarah was closest, so she hurried over to open it.

The judge stepped inside, a clipboard in hand. He tucked it under his arm, then pulled off a glove with the opposite hand. "Morning, Joanie. Sarah."

I knew that voice. "Pete, how are you this morning?"

"Cold." He lowered his hood. "That coffee I started my morning with at Olde Templeton is long gone."

"Well, here." I reached into the case. "Take a cookie. One for you and all the other judges."

He pursed his lips. "You wouldn't be bribing the judges now, would you?" Then he broke into a wide grin.

"Think of it as a participatory display. These were specially created as a result of the display. Tomte porridge cookies."

He took a few steps in my direction. "I take it you found what you needed in the kids' section?"

"I did, thank you." I passed him the cookies, which I'd put in a pastry bag. "Guess you knew exactly what I needed after all. Figured out the recipe the next day. I think it turned out much better than anything I would have found in the cookbooks."

"So what brought you in this morning if not to get some cookies early?" Sarah asked, coming back around the counter to grab the few baked goods that remained from yesterday to put on our day-old shelf.

Pete tapped his keyboard with a pencil. "I need a name."

Sarah tilted her head to the side. "A name?"

"Yeah for the display window. It's a new thing we rolled out. There will be a separate contest for the names. Most creative, that sort of thing."

Both he and Sarah turned to look at me. so busy trying to figure out what the design was going to be, I'd never really thought of what to call it.

"Cookies for Santa?" I didn't sound too sure of my answer. It wasn't all that creative, but at least it was something.

Sarah quickly followed it up by saying, "With a question mark at the end. Just like how it sounded."

I liked where her mind was going. "Exactly. He's hoping to get one last cookie, but the tomtes are trying to run off with the rest. So it's really a question as to whether he'll get another one or not."

Pete smiled as he wrote the name down. "All right, ladies, that's all I need. Thank you for the cookies." He put back on his hood and glove, then headed out the door. After another minute, the judges left and crossed Founder Street to check out the display at Dawg Pound, the specialty hot dog joint.

"Good call on the question mark aspect," I told Sarah.

She turned, putting her hands on her hips. "You came up with that explanation for it pretty quickly. I'm impressed."

I unlocked the cash register. "We make a good team. What do you say we open a few minutes early for anyone who's already around."

"We *do* make a good team." She walked over to the door, then flipped the sign from *closed* to *open.*

"That reminds me. You want to start working here on Wednesdays?"

"But we're not open on Wednesdays."

I gave her a knowing grin. "Not yet . . ." I explained to her what Libby and I had talked about the night before. Through the window, I watched as the grandmother tapped her grandson on the shoulder. She pointed to the bakery, then dug into her purse.

"Yeah, I mean, the bank probably won't care. If I work for them at all on Wednesdays, it's usually just a half day to help with the business banking."

"Great. I wanted to talk to you first in case Gina and Bryan aren't able to come in. Can't run the kitchen and the shop at the same time by myself."

She nodded. "Got you covered."

Thank goodness for Sarah. I didn't know what I'd do without her.

The shop door opened, and the young teenage boy came inside.

"Good morning!" I chimed, using my happy holiday voice that had just a bit more pep than my standard greeting.

"Please tell me you have some of those cookies you have in the window with the tomtes," he said, rushing to the case. "I have been eyeing all your cookies this week as you added them to the windows, and I have to try this one."

"Sure do. We have plenty. I think they're going to be big sellers today." And hopefully through the winter.

"Well, I'll take two of those—one for me and one for my Grama, we're the more adventurous of the family—and then my mom will have a peanut butter kiss and my dad wants a peppermint one with the candy cane crushed into them."

I ducked down to reach into the case to pull out the cookies he'd ordered, placing each in their own bag to make it easier for everyone to eat as they waited for the parade. "Here you go."

We were already down a third of a tray after giving some to Pete, so Sarah ran back to get more of the porridge cookies as the teen boy and I continued to talk while I rang up his order.

"Do you ever take on interns?" he asked as I handed him back his change.

"I haven't, but I'm still pretty new around here, so I'd never say *never*. Why, you know someone who wants an internship?" I tried suppressing the smile I had, but his enthusiasm before even telling me it was him was infectious, and truthfully, I was excited by the idea too. He'd come in the bakery regularly since we'd opened. This was the most I'd ever talked with him, but his small comments about this cookie or that scone or muffin had clued me into an interest in baking that would be great to have on the team.

"All the juniors at school need to have an internship sometime during the school year. I'm only a freshman, but I want to go to culinary school for baking and pastry when I graduate, so a place like this would make for a great internship."

"I like the sound of that. A lot can happen in two

years, but I have a feeling you'll be working here in no time." I stuck out my hand. "I'm Joanie."

He took his in mine. "Sam. Nice to officially meet you."

"Likewise."

"Great." He held up the bag of cookies. "Well, anyway, I should get back and give everyone these. Are you going to watch the parade?"

"You bet. I'll be right behind you probably. Let me know what you think of the cookie."

"Oh, I will." He turned on his heels and strode back out the door.

"He's a cute kid," Sarah said a moment later as she came in with a tray of cookies. "An internship? That's ambitious."

"How much did you hear?"

"All of it. I didn't want to interrupt, but I figured there was no reason to stop listening." She gave a half shrug. It looked funny thanks to her holding the tray, making me laugh. In a different situation, her snooping might have been bothersome, but I trusted her to know when it wouldn't be appropriate, not that I expected a situation like that to arise in the bakery.

"I think he'll be a great intern. He seemed really enthusiastic."

"He's a good kid. Comes from a nice family. My grandparents, and then just my grandpa, were neighbors with his grandparents before his grandpa died and his grandma moved to the nursing home a year or so back. Good to see her out today. She's adorable." She motioned to the window. "Look at her all bundled up."

The older woman reminded me of my great grandmother, who passed away when she was over a hundred. She always dressed in multiple sweaters too. I was twelve when she died and already seeing ghosts, not that I'd told anyone yet. For a time, she came to visit me as a ghost. Something about enjoying her time here too much and having spent so much time here she didn't want to leave. One day I convinced her by mentioning that she must have had a lot of people waiting for her because she had been so old. She'd not really thought about them, I guess, or was more worried about how we'd all be without her.

For the next half hour, there was a rush of people in the bakery, keeping both Sarah and me busy. Everyone wanted to grab something to snack on for the parade. I got many compliments

"Oh, looks like the parade is getting ready to start. Everyone's heads just turned toward the top of the street," Sarah announced.

When we could hear the Heartwood Hollow band begin their marching tune, Sarah and I took it as our cue to close until the end of the parade. As I'd expected, she watched from the window as I headed outside . . . with my coat on this time.

Sam turned, likely hearing the door to the shop open and close. He stood and trotted over to me.

"That cookie was amazing. Was that rice mixed in with the oats?"

"It was. I'm impressed with your ability to pick out ingredients."

"And the buttercream on top of the porridge cookie. Great nod to the tradition."

"You picked up on that, huh?"

"He nodded. I remember reading the stories when I was a kid after they first showed up."

"Any idea where they came from?"

"Not a clue. It must be magic."

I raised an eyebrow at him. "Magic?"

He quirked a grin. "Yeah, you know, Christmas magic? It is that time of year."

I shook my head slowly, my gaze going toward the sky at the cheesy comment. It was rather cute. At that moment, the flag twirlers came into view, the color guard leading the way for the entire parade as the purple flags bearing the image of the Heartwood Hollow Hellcats' mascot swished this way and that and flipped over their bearers' heads and around their bodies. The dramatics sent Sam rushing back to his seat, preventing me from saying anything more.

The parade carried on for forty-five minutes. Floats from various organizations decked out on the backs of trucks or driven by themselves. All colorful. Antique cars that could make an appearance because the snow had not yet fallen. Even members of the high school and community choruses had gotten together to sit on a hayride wagon. They stopped every so often to sing another Christmas carol.

Heartwood Hollow didn't hold back when it came to the holidays or town pride. There were people dressed as trees followed by lumberjacks carrying probably real axes. Children in the scouting groups followed them.

It was a sight to be seen, and it was all capped off by the grand finale. Santa's arrival on a sleigh pulled by a team of reindeer, because of course Heartwood Hollow had reindeer. A farm just outside of town had a herd. They made most of their money at Christmas time renting out the animals and their antique sleighs for events just like this. The reindeer made an appearance at nearly every holiday event where Santa was. It was unique, that was for sure, and the kids loved it.

Truthfully, so did I.

It was, well, magical.

The float in front of Santa's sleigh had large gray sheets draped over it to make it look like it had been sculpted into a mountain range. Fake trees lined the slopes of the mountains, which were capped with white sheets to give an appearance of snowy mountain peaks. When it stopped to accommodate the chorus singing another carol, something under one of the sheets shifted, sending a few trees toppling over. The two riders on top of the float, dressed as Santa's elves, tried their best to corral the falling trees, but in the process, one elf slipped. There was a collective gasp from the parade-goers as we watched the elf grab whatever he could to steady himself. The sheet shifted more as he took hold of it, revealing the Styrofoam peaks that had formed the mountain peaks. And a whole lot more too. Underneath the sheet were all the things that had been presumed stolen in town. The books, the dog statue, Libby's urn, and the apron and hat from Mr. Salvatore's Italian chef statue.

The elves on the float and in the truck pulling the

now crime scene, seemed just as surprised as anyone that the missing objects had been under there.

But as the carolers finished their song a couple floats up, either unaware of what had happened or persevering through the gasp that escaped from those who had seen what happened, the carolers' truck started back up, and the parade continued, heralding Santa's arrival. Several people were on their cell phones either taking pictures or talking. I hoped someone had thought to call the police. I glanced back into the shop. Sarah had disappeared from the door where she'd been watching. Peering around my display, I spotted her on our telephone. Hopefully she'd had the same idea I did.

Locked into the parade procession, the team of elves and their float turned evidence, had nowhere else to go except to follow along with the rest of the route. At least until they could turn off onto a side street, a police officer waving them over.

Libby would be thrilled to have her urn back. How had someone even gotten it up there? How had everything gone unnoticed?

I'd have to ask Seth, Courtney's boyfriend and a first-year police officer with the Heartwood Hollow Police Department.

What would likely be the talk of the town after this was pushed away from everyone's minds, at least momentarily, as the jingling of sleighbells drew our attention. I'd been told that Santa was always positioned immediately behind the elves but as children grew excited to see him and the reindeer, he hung back, soaking in the moment and letting the few courageous kids come up to pet the deer with the help of the reindeer farm's owners who dressed up for the occasion. It put Santa a good distance behind the rest of the parade.

I wondered if he knew what had happened or if he'd been too far back or distracted from seeing it. As he came to a stop in front of the bakery and the little park where his cottage sat, he gave no indication of anything being wrong. He waved at the crowd, bellowing a hearty "Ho ho ho" before nodding to let the few anxious children come up to the reindeer, guided to a different one than had been pet at Santa's last stop. For the rest of the day, at least two of the deer would be penned near the cottage, allowing anyone who hadn't gotten a chance to pet them during the parade an opportunity to do so. Like me. I couldn't wait. Give me an animal and I wanted to pet it and make friends.

After a few minutes, Santa continued on his way. He'd loop around River Street and come back up Founder to his cottage. It would be enough time for people to clear out from along the route and for the farmers to unhitch the reindeer from the sleigh.

At first, no one moved as Santa left. I think we were still too surprised at what had happened with the reveal of the stolen goods. But finally, the swell of people from earlier in the parade route reached us, breaking the magical hold the parade and the unexpected turn of events had over us.

I gave Sam a quick wave as I headed back into the shop, ready to serve cookies to all those looking for a sweet treat and hoping that someone would be able to explain what had just happened.

CHAPTER 13

Something seemed off as I approached the bakery the next morning, but I couldn't figure out what exactly. It wasn't until I'd set foot inside that I realized what was missing.

And what had been found.

My window display—my honorable mention window display—had changed drastically overnight.

The gnomes were gone. Both of the tomtes had somehow disappeared overnight. As had *all* of the oatmeal porridge cookies that had been in the windows. Even the cookie that had been sitting on the plexiglass circle meant to look like Santa was using magic to get it was missing. The other kinds of cookies I'd used in the window display were untouched. We'd sold out yesterday of all cookies right at the end of the day, so there were none in the cases to worry about.

I ran over to the cash register, and even though it was still locked, I opened it to be sure that nothing had been taken. Everything was accounted for. Then I investigated what was sitting on the plate that the cookies had been on, the one that the tomtes had been holding.

It was a small blue velvet box, the kind one gets from a jewelry store. I picked it up, cautious in case it wasn't what I thought it was.

Upon opening the little box, I discovered a ring. A diamond ring. Just like I'd suspected.

I'd spoken with Drew yesterday when he and Megan stopped by after the parade. She'd been beaming, clearly in the holiday spirit. He was too, in a way, but he had hoped to propose to her last night, and that knowledge couldn't have been easy to hold on to when the ring had yet to be found.

This had to be the missing ring. But how was it here?

We'd cleaned everything when he first reported that he'd lost it, quite possibly in the shop. But now, here it was sitting in the jewelry box I assumed it came in. And this was definitely not a spot where it could have been before.

So who had put the ring here, and who had taken the cookies and the tomtes?

This went way beyond what I believed any high school senior could do as part of a prank. That was what yesterday's spectacle had been determined to be, even before the investigation was over. A senior prank for the holidays. Some in town had thought that when the apron and hat had first gone missing from the chef statue in front of Salvatore's, saying it had happened before. Stay, the dog statue, was easy enough for a high schooler to grab unnoticed. The books from the library statue too. But there had to have been several people involved for something like Libby's urn to have gone missing. That was massive.

As it turned out, many people were responsible.

Steph became my inside source for all this information once we settled down to grab dinner back at the apartment before the evening festivities continued. She told me that the short-lived investigation revealed that several of the seniors involved drove trucks for the lumber company and had the proper equipment to move Libby's urn.

This was probably the most elaborate prank I'd ever seen. Way more so than anything my high school had ever cooked up.

The elves on the float as well as the two inside the truck pulling it hadn't seen the stuff underneath the sheet until the incident. They'd been under the impression that only pillows and Styrofoam forms had been used to create the mountain range to the northwest of Heartwood Hollow that gave the landscape its rolling hills out toward Bug Creek and Knoll's Grove. And most of it was, but not all of it. So it was a shock when the elf grabbed the sheet to keep from falling, revealing Libby's urn in the process. Based on where everything was revealed to be once the sheet was removed, it was either the hat or the apron that had caused the elf to slip in the first place. Mr. Salvatore seemed pleased that his stuff had helped reveal the whole plot, and when he learned that it was his police report preventing the release of everyone's things, he quickly stated that he wouldn't press charges against a group of kids. Once the others who'd had things taken said the same, the police returned everyone's possessions. None were so happy as Mr. Sal and Clara, who tightly held Stay to her chest as she walked off toward her house.

Even more than what I had known about had been taken too. Other lawn ornaments, including a birdbath, were also found amongst the padding of the float. Once the discovery was made, several townspeople reported things that had gone missing over the last week, and most were able to reclaim their possessions. But a couple things reported after the fact weren't found on the float, including one of those glass gazing balls with the oily exteriors. Neither were some glass suncatcher wind chimes off someone else's porch.

The few seniors who admitted to the thefts swore they hadn't taken those few things, saying everything they took was on the truck so that it could all go back to its owners after the reveal. They'd had something else planned for that, but the elf falling was an unexpected change of plans. Fortunately for them—and Alex—the seniors' cooperation in the investigation as well as every-one's refusal to charge them with theft meant that the few football players who were involved got to suit up for the game. That's all Alex let them do, though. Both he and the coach were furious. Almost didn't let the guys have my muffins. The team scraping out a win by some-thing called *a field goal*, however, brightened up both their spirits. I already had a muffin order for the next game.

So was the senior prank at all related to what happened with my window display? The missing tomtes fit part of the pattern, but then again, all the tomtes from around the cottage had moved overnight as they usually did. And the stuff the students had taken had all been outside. Coming into the bakery would have elevated what they did to beyond a prank. It didn't make sense to do it after they'd already been found out either.

I still had questions, but I wasn't sure I'd ever find out the answers. What about the stuff I'd heard about being stolen in the last few years while I was shopping the other day? Was that related at all? And why of all things would someone have put the ring in the tomtes' place? It was likely the most valuable item whoever had it could have taken. Had they gotten nervous and decided to get rid of it when they came into the bakery?

I'd been told upon moving here that Heartwood Hollow was safe. That I didn't need to lock my apartment or secure my bike when I made deliveries or when it sat behind the bakery during the day. Coming from college in a city where I lived in busy dorms and later in an apartment inside a triple-decker, common urban worker housing where I'd gone to school, locking doors was a requirement. Break-ins weren't common, but when they happened, they were much larger than a pile of books that couldn't even be read.

It crossed my mind to have cameras installed when I opened the bakery. No one else seemed to have them, though, and everyone I'd talked to about it had said it was unnecessary. Heartwood Hollow wasn't like that.

I didn't want to be that one business that did and set myself apart. I wanted to fit in with the town, not be different. The rumors about me set me apart enough as it was.

But had I put up cameras, I'd at least have known how all the porridge cookies disappeared along with the tomtes. It's not like they took off on their own. They didn't even have legs.

But what if the thieves didn't have bodies in the traditional sense either? I hadn't considered the possibility of ghosts being behind the stolen things around town, and I'd discounted them from moving all the tomtes, but just the two from my shop and the cookies seemed like a possibility. It wouldn't be the first time they'd messed with me.

I wondered if I should call the police to report this, but nothing of value had been taken. I would never be able to sell those cookies anyway, so it wasn't like I'd had a saleable product stolen either. And the tomtes weren't even mine. Technically, I'd taken them. And if a ghost were responsible, what good would the police do? I'd wait and see what Sarah thought when she got in. If anyone could convince me to call, it would be her. I wouldn't bring up my ghost theory, though. That, along with the secret of my being able to see ghosts, was staying with me.

I looked at the clock on the wall above the back counter. It was early. Really early. Drew worked in the office of the Phoenix Foundation at the far end of Main Street. It was through his work there that I'd met him. The foundation provided funds for the development and enhancement of Heartwood Hollow and the surrounding region, and I'd been given money to help pay for the bakery's renovations. Drew had helped me prepare the lengthy grant proposal. If memory served me right, he'd be heading into the office for eight. I'd give him a call about the ring just before that so maybe I'd catch him on the way to work. Oh, would he be surprised!

Carefully, I closed the ring box and then slipped it into my apron pocket. I didn't take my apron off for anything. Not even to make deliveries. The ring would stay with me until Drew came to get it himself.

This was going to be the longest few hours of my life.

Moments later, I heard Gina and Bryan come in from the back entrance.

"We're going to need to make an extra half batch of the porridge cookies today," I told my drowsy bakers as I walked into the kitchen to greet them.

"Only a half?" Bryan asked through a yawn. The town festivities had run until late at night and no doubt they'd been up at least as late as I had celebrating at River View Park with music and hot chocolate and dancing. Well, I wasn't dancing. There was no need to make a fool of myself for that. I didn't trust my feet. Never had.

"Yeah, I have to replace the ones from the display. Eh, make it a full batch. It's Sunday. We'll get the foot traffic in."

Gina raised an eyebrow. "What happened to the cookies in the display?"

I shrugged. "They disappeared." As we set up our workstations for the morning, I told them how I'd found the bakery when I first walked in, including finding the missing wedding ring that had to belong to Drew. "So what do you two think? Should I call the police?"

"No," Gina answered at the same time as Bryan

shook his head. "It's more important to get Drew his ring."

"You don't want it to get held up as evidence," Bryan added.

I pursed my lips. They had a point. Although Drew would likely be relieved that the ring had been found and that he knew where it was while it was in police custody, I didn't want to delay him any more than he had been already with proposing to Megan.

"I guess you're right." I would, however, call a locksmith to have the locks replaced. At least that way I'd know whoever had gotten inside wouldn't be able to again. Unless it had been a ghost, of course. They didn't have to use doors if they didn't want to.

Bryan and Gina exchanged a glance. "We are," they said in unison.

"Just chalk it up to a little Christmas magic, is all," Gina added.

I nodded. Overall, the idea of magic being behind this was silly, but given the time of year, maybe I could accept that explanation. Just this once. After all, hadn't I been playing to that theme with my window display?

At seven forty-five, I picked up the bakery phone and called Drew at the number he'd left when he first told us the ring was missing.

"Hello?" He sounded half-asleep.

Drats, I'd forgotten it was Sunday. He was probably just as tired as we all were after the holiday festivities if not more so. He was still dancing away with Megan when Steph, Alex, and I walked home.

"I'm so sorry, Drew, I must have woken you."

"Who is this?"

"It's Joanie from Suncraft Bakery."

"Joanie?"

"Yes, I'm calling because I think we have something here that you are going to want." I hoped he could hear the smile in my voice.

He perked up at that, and when he responded, "I'll be there in fifteen," he sounded more alert.

I removed the box from my apron the moment he stepped into the shop. "I think this belongs to you."

His head tilted in question as he took the box from me and opened it. "This is the ring. Oh my goodness, you found it. Where was it?"

I explained to him the missing tomtes and cookies. "It was right there on the plate where the cookies should have been."

"This is amazing. But—"

"But what?"

"I don't understand how you have the box the ring came in too. Did you just have one lying around?"

I shook my head. "The ring was inside the box. Why?"

"I never had the box with me. I'd been carrying the ring around in my pants pocket. I threw the box somewhere that Megan wouldn't find it, in my desk drawer at work. I knew if I kept it at home, she'd end up putting my socks away or something and find it there."

My eyes widened as my shoulder lifted slightly. "I don't know what to tell you. This is exactly how I found it. Box and all." Maybe this whole Christmas magic idea had something going for it after all.

"This is the strangest thing. But thank you so much. I may have had my opportunity last night ruined, but at least I have the ring now for when the moment is right."

I felt bad for him for losing his chance last night, but maybe he could do it today. I sized Drew up. He looked to be about the same size as the man who had played Santa for the town yesterday at the cottage on the parade. "What if you could get a new opportunity sooner than you thought?"

He quirked an eyebrow. "Like how soon?"

"You doing anything this evening? I have an idea."

Over the next half hour, I told him my thoughts, and he and I fleshed them out a bit more. We now had a plan, all right, but I was going to need a little help to help pull it off.

CHAPTER 14

The morning crawled by despite the heavy foot traffic. There was too much anticipation in the air, and the bakery seemed overly bright, but that was probably a play on the angle of the sun and my antsyness. Not only did I have Drew's upcoming proposal to play a part in, but I had the open house to go to at one as well.

"Good luck!" Sarah said as I came back into the shop, putting on my coat.

"Thanks. I have a really good feeling about this one."

She chuckled. "Like you do about your couples?"

I cracked a smile. That was how I tried to play my matchmaking off when it happened. As if I had a good feeling about the couple. Now I was using it to describe me and a house. Only there was no tingling sensation like there was with people.

"Maybe I should become a realtor."

Sarah shook her finger at me slowly, a smirk on her face. "Maybe you should. Bet you'd get a lot of commissions if you're as good at matching people to houses as you are to other people."

I wrapped my scarf around my neck, tucking the ends into my coat before zipping it up. "Matching, huh?"

"Yeah, you're a matchmaker. No doubt about it. People have seen Whitney and Xavier together all week, and the story of you introducing them is already going around. I think the idea of a matchmaking baker is going to stick."

I shrugged, not wanting to seem too hung up on the idea. Donna had used the same term to describe me a few days ago. "It kinda has a ring to it, I guess."

"Speaking of rings, you figure out what you're going to say to Megan to get her to Santa's cottage?"

"I'll figure it out on my walk back." I pulled on my hat, followed by my gloves.

Sarah's eyes grew wide. "You're walking?"

"I could ride my bike, I guess."

She shivered. "It's so cold."

"Best time to figure out if I'm going to like the walk to the shop and back if I do get the house. Imagine how much nicer it will be when the weather is perfect." And the weather today wasn't bad. It was only cold. Not wet or windy.

"Better you than me." Looking to the ceiling, she shook her head slowly.

"See you in a bit!"

I rushed out the door and immediately crossed Main Street to head up Founder past Leafs and Grounds. My addiction to marshmallow rice treats would not go away if this were my path to and from work, but I wasn't looking to eliminate them from my diet anytime soon. The bank was also up this street, which would make putting in the business deposits easier. We wouldn't need to make special trips just for that anymore.

I continued up a ways before seeing the house on the corner. Several cars were already parked along the street on this side. Another few on the other side. A couple of people were in the house's backyard as I approached. I could hear them talking about what they'd need to do to the house if they were to get it. Funny, to me, the house didn't need anything on the outside. Not on the inside, either, based on the pictures I had seen once Kathy sent me the listing. Granted I'd been using my phone in the stairwell of my building to look at them because of my apartment's shoddy Wi-Fi and cell service, but still.

I turned the corner to find even more people parked along that street. Wow. At no other open house that I had been to had there been this many cars.

"Don't let all the cars fool you," Kathy said as she stepped out of her vehicle. Guess they're having some sort of a party a couple houses down. There really aren't that many people inside. Some, though, so let's come on."

I sighed with relief. I didn't want to have to go up against people in a bidding war. I doubted I would win. My grandfather had left me some money in a trust, but it was running low. It was how I'd gotten the bakery up and running, covering what a couple of small business loans and a grant from the Phoenix Foundation couldn't, but the house's asking price was all I could afford to mortgage. I couldn't go higher.

Kathy and I shook hands as I said, "Thanks for meeting me today."

She nodded. "Of course. We gotta find you a house, and hopefully this one is it. You seemed so excited when you first called me about it."

"I don't know." I shrugged. "There's just something about it."

"What are your first impressions?" she asked as we walked up the driveway and onto the small flagstone path leading to the porch.

"It's cute. Perhaps a little bigger than I need for just me, but there's plenty of room for my cat to run around in, and the kitchen looks to be a good size. That is one of the most important things. And there's a bedroom for guests." I thought about having my gram come visit, my mom too. They hadn't been able to stay with me in either of my apartments. But here it wouldn't be a problem.

"And not to mention the porch. According to the paperwork, the swing stays."

I glanced up at the white porch swing and choked down a laugh, covering it with a cough. Tomtes.

Kathy turned toward me, concerned. "You okay?"

"Yeah." I pointed to the swing.

She glanced over, and a smile appeared on her face. "Looks like the realtor was trying to add a little whimsy to the showing today."

"You think the realtor did it?" Momentarily thinking that she meant moving all the tomtes throughout town before coming to my senses. I wondered if this realtor was the same as the one who had lined the tomtes along the walkway of the other house for sale that I had passed the other day.

"These here? Oh sure. They're all around town. Easy enough to grab some and move them about with how often they get scattered this way and that."

I nodded. "That makes sense." With the way everyone was moving them—even me—anyone in Heartwood Hollow could have been responsible for taking the two out of my shop. I would probably never find out who was behind moving them, or who had started it anyway.

As we got closer to the porch, I could clearly see the several gnomes who were sitting on the swing.

"Hey, I know you." The tomte with posable arms was no worse for the wear, minus a few crumbs still on his beard. I imagined him taking a bite out of the cookies he'd spent all of yesterday staring at. As silly as it was, I liked that version of events better than someone taking him and the cookies. It went better with the Christmas magic theory. "How did you get all the way out here?"

"Friend of yours?" Kathy chuckled.

"He'd been a part of my window display," I said, brushing the cookie crumbs off his beard before setting him back down on the swing. "He was gone this morning."

"Oh no! Did someone break in?"

"No, not at all. I have no idea how the two tomtes managed to leave along with all the cookies that I'd put in the display window yesterday." I scanned the swing. "The second tomte that I had isn't here, though."

Seemingly satisfied with being told that no one had

broken in, she didn't question me further and replied, "You had a very cute window."

"Thanks."

"Now, shall we go in?"

I nodded, giving the tomtes one last look before gently nudging the swing to send it in a light rocking motion. Nothing too strong. The tomtes had weighted bottoms, but I didn't want them to fall over with too much of a push.

Kathy opened the door, then stepped inside, holding it open for me so I could do the same. We were in the living room, and I could see straight on into the kitchen through an open archway. There looked like maybe there had once been a door, or at least half of one across the lower portion of the opening, but nothing separated the two spaces anymore.

The room was a good size with a fireplace at the other end, a mantle over it. The stairs going up were to the side of that, angling back overhead, creating a nook under the stairs that would be great for a bookshelf. I could see putting one in the fireplace too since I didn't see myself using it for its intended purpose. And Saffy would love her spot on the back of the couch even more with it pushed up against the bay window overlooking the porch and front yard.

"To the side here, you have a little bit of a bonus room. Maybe a mudroom or a kids' playroom," Kathy said, preventing me from going into interior decorating mode any more than I already had.

I poked my head into the room as I took off my gloves and then stuffed them into my pockets. Kids weren't on my radar at this point in my life, so a mudroom would work. But the room would fit my rarely used computer and desk that hung out in a corner of my apartment.

"So do you want to see the bedrooms upstairs first or the kitchen?"

"Bedrooms. We can come back downstairs after and do the kitchen and backyard." I wanted to save what I hoped would be the best for last.

"Great. One big loop." Kathy led the way up the stairs, and once we got to the top, said, "To your right here, is the bathroom."

I was excited that it had a bathtub and a shower. Both of my apartments only had shower stalls due to the small space. I envisioned getting one of those bathtub boards to go across the tub in front of me where I could put a candle, my tea, some chocolates, and a book so I could sit and soak until the water got cold if that was what I wanted.

Next to the bathroom was a linen closet, and past that at the end of the hall was one of the bedrooms.

"This is the smaller of the two bedrooms, but I know some people have a preference of looking out over the front yard versus the back. I'd say the front of the house is usually the louder side, being closer to the road, especially with this house being on a corner, but—" she chuckled "—it's Heartwood Hollow. You know the noise level around here."

She meant very little. Especially once you got off the main roads.

"This would make a great guest room."

She nodded. "Fair enough. Let's go see what would be your bedroom, then."

We stepped back into the hallway, and she pointed up to a rectangular panel in the ceiling. "That would be your access to the attic. Want to take a look? There should be stairs."

Never very fond of attics, I shook my head. It's where ghosts tended to hang out who wanted to stick around and possibly try to haunt something. Fortunately, the house felt ghost-free, which was nice.

Still, I didn't want to go into the attic. "Saw the pictures. It will make a good storage space." I'd be sure to have the building inspector make sure everything up there was fine before any paperwork was signed.

"I've never been much of a fan of them myself," Kathy said. "Even the ones with full staircases going up to them. Usually hot and either muggy or musty. Bad for my allergies."

I nodded in acknowledgment, then led the way into the larger of the two bedrooms. It was a good five or six feet wider than the guest bedroom with plenty of room for my queen bed and dresser. My mirror too.

Kathy flipped a page of the small stack of papers she was holding before pointing to an open doorway in the corner of the room. "There's a small three-quarter bath over there, with just a toilet, sink, and shower stall, not that you're too far away from the other bathroom. Comes in handy, though. Wish I had two bathrooms. Then I wouldn't always have to wait on my daughter." She chuckled. "Or her on me."

I peeked into the closet next to the bathroom, which

was a decent size with double sliding doors and a built-in single drawer at the base of the closet and a shelf over the bar where I'd hang my clothes. I had an armoire too, but this would allow me to swap clothes out with the seasons . . . or maybe put the nice clothes in the armoire. I didn't really see myself as the type to rotate my wardrobe, even with the additional room. Besides, I tended to keep a lot of the things the same, like my t-shirts that I'd put a cardigan or a sweatshirt over to layer. And when I wasn't in the bakery, I was a leggings and jeans all-year-round type of person.

"It has a great view of the backyard too," Kathy added.

I peeked out the window. It wasn't a huge backyard but big enough to have friends over for cookouts and the like. I'd need to have Steph and Alex over regularly. I'd miss living so close to the two of them. Courtney and Seth, too, now that I'd have the space.

"You ready to see the kitchen?"

"Yes. Absolutely."

Trailing behind Kathy, I made sure that the stairs were as easy going down as coming up. Klutzy me needed a sturdy handrail and wide steps, especially with only having a bathroom upstairs. That meant added trips up and down each day.

But all was good once I reached the living room. I felt comfortable that I could manage the stairs without looking and being conscious of every step.

"I think you're going to like this," Kathy said, already in the kitchen.

As I turned the corner at the entryway, the kitchen

came into full view. My smile grew so wide I could feel it in my ears.

Kathy chuckled. "Oh, you more than like."

"It's wonderful." Easily double the size of my current kitchen if not more. Except for the sink, counter space ran along one entire wall, ending at the door to the backyard. Plus, there were a few more feet between the stove and the refrigerator. The cupboards were all at a decent height, and I'd be able to reach the top shelf of the upper cabinets with only a little step stool.

"Probably the only downside is the fact you wouldn't have a dining room here. I imagine that, with you being a baker, a lot of holiday dinners will be at your house."

"I don't have a big family. There's plenty of room for a table." I peeked under the sink. No evidence of leaks new or old. "Maybe I'll get one with a leaf I can add in when I need another spot."

"Then it sounds perfect."

It really did. I ran my fingers across the countertop and along the edge of the sink as I made my way to the back door.

The yard was empty when we went outside. We must have missed the other group leave while we were upstairs. The only things out here now were a few more tomtes sitting on the steps to a small shed at the back of the house. Bonus. I hadn't seen that from the window. The whole yard was bigger than it had seemed when I looked outside. It could easily fit more than the several friends I'd made here so far.

"It's a great fenced-in lot. Tons of potential," Kathy explained. "There is a gate to the neighbor's yard, but

George is a sweetheart, so I'm sure he wouldn't mind if you wanted to get a normal section of fence in there."

If George was a sweetheart, then there was no need for a normal section of fence. I was fine with the gate. It wasn't like he was going to randomly come into my backyard. Besides, the gate gave the backyard character. There was a side gate too that led to the sidewalk. I bet that would make any sort of gathering back here easier. Less foot traffic through the house. Saffy would appreciate that.

We didn't stay too long in the backyard. It was cold, and besides the shed, which I quickly peeked into, finding only a few basic yard tools, there wasn't much to see. Back inside, I only had one thing to say to Kathy.

"Put a bid in."

CHAPTER 15

On the way back from the open house, I stopped off a Santa's cottage to hopefully put Drew's and my plan into motion. A line wrapped around the corner of the street, an elf stationed halfway and at the end of the line. It was a decent weekend job for the teenagers in town to make a few extra bucks for the holiday season.

I recognized one of the elves as a regular customer and approached her. "Hey, Lauren, how's it going today?"

"Good!" The high school junior pinched the top of her green ensemble with white tights. "Thank goodness most of this is fleece though, or else it might be a little cold."

"Any chance I might be able to get Santa's help during the dinner break?"

She tilted her head, then perked up to wave at a child in line. "What do you need St. Nick for?"

"Well, truthfully, it isn't so much St. Nick that I need . . . I would like to borrow his suit."

"The one in your window not enough for you?"

I'd considered it but was hesitant to get rid of my window display so early in the season. Plus, it had been hard enough to put up on my own. I wasn't ready to try to take it down, even with some help this time.

I chuckled. "I need the cottage too."

"Oh, this sounds interesting. What for?" She turned to answer a parent's question about taking pictures before pivoting back to me for my answer.

"I'm hoping to help a friend with a proposal."

"Like, a marriage proposal?"

I nodded, and her eyes grew wide with excitement.

"Let me go check with Santa."

She darted away, and I followed several feet behind her to watch as Lauren first checked in with the elf inside the cottage. I wondered if they rotated line duty. It was warmer looking in there. After a moment, that elf nodded her head.

When Santa was done with the child who had been on his lap, Lauren quickly scooted up toward his chair and whispered something in his ear. He whispered something back, and she pointed to me before saying something else. He gave me a thumbs-up, and Lauren hurried back to me.

"He gets an hour for dinner starting right at five. The cottage is usually locked up, but he'll stop in the bakery with the key. He says he wants a porridge cookie."

Laughing, I said, "I think I can make that happen."

"He'd also appreciate the use of your bathroom to change out of the suit. Something about character continuity. They'll see him go in as Santa, and then your friend will come out as Santa, and the same goes for later when he needs to change back into the suit. He usually goes home to eat so no one sees him out of costume."

I clasped my hands together. "Great. All of this sounds completely doable."

"If you need any help, I'm more than willing to stay through the break. I would kind of love to see the proposal happen."

"You know? We just might have need of an elf, thanks."

"I've never seen a marriage proposal before." She beamed. "Oh, I'm so excited."

Even with my track record of matching couples together, I'd only seen a couple. One was at a restaurant with friends. The other at a baking competition. The third wasn't even one of my couples. I'd just happened to be there at the right time to witness the moment.

"Me too, Lauren. Me too."

Drew showed up at four thirty. Nervous but excited energy radiated off him as he paced my shop. After several minutes, I sent him back into the kitchen with a cookie. I checked in on him a few minutes later, and he was sitting on an overturned milk crate munching away. Cookies made everything better, even pre-proposal jitters.

Right at five, Santa walked into the bakery carrying a velvet drawstring bag about the size of a backpack. We were still open, having taken up extended hours for the holiday season, but there weren't any customers in the shop at the moment.

"Ho ho ho!" he exclaimed, giving me a wave.

"Hello, Santa!" Truth was, I didn't know who was in the suit and had nothing else to call him.

"I hear you're in need of a suit. Just point me in the direction of your bathroom and it's all yours for—" he pulled a giant pocket watch from out of his vest pocket "—oh, about forty-five minutes."

Just enough time.

"Great. The bathroom is through the kitchen on the left. Once you're out of the suit, if you could give it to the gentleman waiting in there, he's going to be the one using it."

He gave me a thumbs-up as he strode into the kitchen. A few minutes later, the man who had been in the suit returned in normal clothes. I smiled, recognizing who he was now as one of Donna's early morning customers. Despite lacking a white beard of his own—he was still more pepper than salt on his head too—with the fake Santa beard on and what must have been a padded suit, he was perfect for the roll. Even as a snarky diner customer hungry for breakfast, both he and his best friend exuded the warmth that any good Santa required.

"Ah, that's better," Paul said. "Now I can go grab something from Dawg Pound. I usually have to go home to keep up the ruse or one of the elves has to pick something up for me."

"Well, take this before you go. And then you can

have dessert when you're done." I passed him a white paper bag with a porridge cookie in it. "I'm surprised you didn't ask for a muffin."

"Aww, those are special for breakfast. Walter would never forgive me if I had one without him. But cookies are for any time." He held up the bag. "Thanks, Joanie. I look forward to hearing about this proposal. I already wished Drew good luck."

"Thanks. Enjoy your dinner. I'll see you in a little bit."

He headed out the door, passing none other than Megan on her way in. My heart jumped in my throat. I should have known she'd be early. And based on the tingling sensation flowing from my toes to my stomach, Drew was still in the kitchen, hopefully fully changed into the Santa suit.

"Megan, how are you? What brings you in this evening?"

"Hey, Joanie. Sarah. Good to see you both again. Drew called and said he wanted me to pick up an order for him."

"Ah, that's right." I turned toward Sarah, raising my brows at her when I was sure Megan couldn't see. "Would you mind going and grabbing that box from the kitchen? I think there's a note on it."

"Can do," she replied before hurrying out from behind the counter and sneaking into the kitchen, careful to not let the door swing open too much to possibly ruin the surprise and then pushing the door closed behind her so it wouldn't stay open longer than it had to.

Judging from Megan's relaxed demeanor as she waited, she had no idea what was in store for her in just a few short minutes. She asked me how I was doing and how I was enjoying my first Christmas season with the bakery, hopefully not noticing the extra time Sarah was taking in the back.

It took several moments, but as the tingling sensation of having a match close by lessened, Sarah returned to the shop with the box, a red and green ribbon already tied around it. She pulled a sticky note from its top. "Says it's already paid."

I nodded. "Drew took care of it over the phone earlier."

"Well, that's good," Megan said. "I wasn't planning to have to come here until he called to ask me to, so having to pay wouldn't have been a pleasant surprise. Although I half-expected it. He's been acting so strange this last week. Jumpy. You should have seen him every time the phone rang. And then this morning he got a call while I was making coffee, and he jetted out the door. I haven't seen him since."

His nerves were probably shot after this week of having lost the ring and now with getting ready to propose. I didn't say any of that out loud, though. "Men are so strange sometimes."

We shared a laugh about that as Sarah passed the box over to Megan.

"You've got that right," Megan said. She lifted a piece of paper on the box, then looked at me, a skeptical gleam in her eye. "And sometimes they keep getting stranger. Now I'm supposed to deliver this to Santa's cottage next door." She raised an eyebrow. "You two couldn't offer a delivery option when it's right there?"

I shrugged. "Like you said, men are strange. I offered and he said no."

She shook her head, and her skepticism was replaced with a slightly forced but pleasant smile plastered across her face. Soon enough, a real smile would overtake that one once she realized what was happening. "All right, well, I'm going to go bring some Christmas cheer to Santa and his elves. Thanks, Joanie."

"You're welcome. Have a good evening!"

She left the shop, and I spun toward Sarah.

Before I could say anything, she held her hand up. "Helped him finish getting into his suit and sent him out the back door."

With a sigh of relief that Drew was all set and hadn't run out of the bakery half in the suit, I headed toward the kitchen door. "Thanks. Shall we go peek in on the proposal?"

She arched a brow, her eyes widening. "What about the shop?"

"We're right next door. Everything will be fine for a few minutes."

She rushed to follow me, and I handed over her jacket once I beat her to the closet. We threw our coats on and were still in the process of getting them zipped up as we watched Megan try to hand the box of cookies to Lauren, the Santa's cottage camera around her neck.

Megan seemed hesitant to follow Lauren at first when she refused to take the box, but Megan finally relented. At the door to the cottage, she bent over in laughter, holding her stomach with one hand and the box with the other. Drew must not have been as convincing of a Santa as Paul was.

Sarah and I rushed to the cottage window to peek through it as Megan stepped inside, Lauren following her, camera at the ready.

Megan passed Santa the box of cookies, saying something that we couldn't hear. Lauren was already snapping photos.

Drew placed the box on the small table next to him beside a scroll Santa used to show kids if they were on the naughty or nice list. When their name wasn't on it, Santa would say there was still time to go one way or the other and followed it with something motivational about being kind and helpful. One of the parents had explained it to me yesterday after taking her son to see Santa before coming into the shop.

Drew tapped his lap, and Megan, still chuckling, sat on his leg. I wondered if she had any idea what was going to happen at this point. He was talking, and she nodded. I imagined him asking her if she had been good this year and her saying yes. He took the scroll and together they looked at the names. Drew gave a big nod as he tapped the list, likely finding her name. He rolled the scroll up before putting it aside.

Then he made a show of feeling around in his vest pockets before having Megan stand. He checked his pants pockets and then held up a finger as if remembering something. He reached into the Santa jacket that hung from a hook next to the oversized chair.

Drew pulled out the ring box, then turned toward Megan, dropping onto one knee as he did.

Her hands flew up to cover her mouth, but they couldn't hide her smile as he opened the box, and they didn't muffle her resounding yes as she accepted his marriage proposal. Her answer had been so loud we could hear it from where we were watching.

Drew stood after sliding the ring onto her finger, and Megan threw her arms around him.

Something cold landed on my cheek and dissipated quickly. Then another and another.

As if by some Christmas magic aided by a little magic called love, it had started snowing in Heartwood Hollow.

CHAPTER 16

I sat on my couch drinking a cup of tea that tasted like sugar cookies. It was Tuesday, my day off. My *one* day off a week now that I'd be opening the bakery on Wednesdays thanks to my partnership with Libby to bake for all her tea services.

Today I refused to get off my couch until I absolutely had to. Later, I'd meet up with Steph and Alex for dinner. Then we'd go see the carolers that were performing on the Town Hall lawn. During the week, all of the town's holiday events were at night. Next weekend promised to be even more jam-packed with activities, although I believed Santa Claus getting engaged as the first snow of the season fell would be the highlight of this year's festivities.

It was the talk of the town almost immediately. Lauren had gotten some great pictures, and the couple was quick to post them to social media to announce their engagement.

Monday, several people came to the bakery wanting

to hear more details once they heard about the shop's part in making it happen. No doubt this only added to the rumors about me. Everyone in town loved their gossip.

Saffy lay on my feet as I read. The phone rang, cutting into the silence of my reading time. She hopped off the couch, clearly offended by the interruption.

I swung my legs down, slipping my feet into my slippers, then stood. "I'll be back on the couch before you know it, Saf. You don't have to go away."

Since my cell phone didn't work in the apartment, I relied on a landline that hung by the door to my unit.

"Hello?"

"Joanie? It's Kathy."

A nervous lump formed in my throat. I hadn't expected to hear back from her so soon. They were having another showing of the house tomorrow. But maybe she'd found another house to look at. "Hey, how are you?"

"Oh, I'm fine. Listen, I'm calling about the house . . . they accepted your offer!"

And just like that, the nervousness melted away only to be replaced by a strange sense of disbelief and excitement.

"You still there?"

"Yes," I said quickly. "Processing it. Wow. That's great!"

"Are you busy? I'm going to need you to come by the office and fill out some paperwork and bring a check for the earnest deposit."

"The bakery is closed on Tuesdays, so I can come

down whenever's convenient."

"I have a showing at three, but other than that, I'll be here all day. Come whenever."

"Fabulous. I'll see you soon."

We hung up, and I turned to see Saffy sitting in front of her food bowls, squinting at me, but it wasn't her content slow-blinking squint. This one was the closest thing to a scowl she could do.

"Now, don't give me that look. I know I told you I'd be back to sit with you in a minute, and I will. It's just going to be a bit longer than that now." I pulled her container of baked tuna treats out from the cupboard, then dropped two in her dish. "We got the house, Saf, the one with the big window I was telling you about. We're moving. You're going to love it."

She said nothing, not that she could actually talk, but lowered her head to have her treats. I took it as my sign that I'd been dismissed.

I was buying a house!

This holiday season was going to get a whole lot busier now, but I was up for it all.

The tomtes will return.

Matchmaking, baking, and ghosts... a recipe for disaster or a spell for success?
Joanie's adventures continue in *Cookies and Curses*, Book One of the Mixing Up Magic series, available now.

What's Next?

Matchmaking, baking, and ghosts... a recipe for disaster or a spell for success?

I've never been wrong with cookies or love, and it's made my bakery popular in my small town. Rumors claim my matchmaking skills come from a dash of magic in my treats, but I can ignore the gossip about me being a witch.

But ghosts only I can see suddenly needing my help? That was never a part of my business plan, and solving their problems might be more than I can handle.

If I can't figure out the mystery of why they're coming between the couples I've connected, then not only will my matches not get their happily ever afters but failing could conjure the end of my livelihood too. I can't let the cookie crumble on my career.

Ghosts, it's time to meet your baker.

Cookies and Curses **is now available.**
Grab it today to continue reading Joanie's magical story.

Acknowledgments

Thank you to my family and friends for their continued support of this dream of mine. To Kahlan, my constant mini-editor, have fun with the clipboard. I'm getting a few more for Christmas and I think you are going to be so excited. To Rob, thank you for putting up with the last-minute rush of publishing as always.

Thank you to my newsletter subscribers who I turned to recently for they help in naming the mascots for the schools in Heartwood Hollow. Deirdrie chose the Hellcats, which won during a newsletter subscriber vote. The reader who chose the Howlers prefers to remain anonymous. Thank you, too, to Darla, who has been fabulous finding those typos that escape multiple rounds of edits and proofreading, for her eagle eyes.

My thanks to the Writing Productivity Challenge, organized by Melissa Storm and Alana Terry, and the wonderful authors who took part and motivated me to power through the end of this book during the September challenge. I was thrilled to come full circle and finish edits during the October challenge.

And finally, thank you to *you* for reading this book.

About the Author

Rosie Pease is a native Rhode Islander but has lived in Vermont, New York, and Ohio. She uses the places she's traveled to as inspiration for the settings of her cozy mysteries, pulling the theater from one, the cider mill from another, the river from another to create a fictitious town that feels familiar.

She collects Funko Pops of the Harry Potter, Hunger Games, Doctor Who, DC TV, and Marvel variety, with a few others thrown in for fun. Her desk is a mess, but she can find everything on it, so it works for her as long as things aren't falling onto the keyboard as she writes.

When she's not crafting cozy mysteries, she's playing with her daughter, hanging out with her husband, or being amused by her two crazy cats.

Come find Rosie online:
Website: https://rosiepease.com
Facebook, Instagram, Twitter, and Pinterest:
@WriteRosiePease

ALSO BY ROSIE PEASE

The Matchmaking Baker

Coffee and Calicos

Sweets and Santa

Mixing Up Magic

Cookies and Curses

Scones and Spells

Weddings and Witchcraft

Potluck and Powers

Purrfect Travel Companion

Catastrophe on the Road

Catastrophe in the Kitchen